The Adventures of James Best
Vol 1
Revelations

Introduction

James Best was born, in my mind and on paper, in 1989. I was 15 years old, going on 16 that year. Our Swedish teacher used to give us different themes to write fiction on. Every time she would tell the class "I want at least 1 A4 page from you all. Except you Tim, please no more than 25 pages." I couldn't promise that. I loved writing, and I loved writing loads of pages. Our teacher used to read a selection of the written fiction and there was one time when she read mine and one of my class mate's stories one after each other. The jury is still out on if she did this to embarrass me or him. The theme for the stories at this time was "A trip to the moon." First she read my class mate's story. It basically consisted of: "10, 9 , 8, 7, 6, 5, 4, 3, 2, 1 blast off! The rocket went to the Moon and we landed safely. We then went home. The end!" Not much more than that. I still remember this vividly as it became a pivotal point in my life when I realised that I might actually have a chance at becoming a writer. Next our teacher read my account on the trip to the Moon. I also included the countdown to blast off, however in between each second I made an account on how the crew was feeling, thoughts running through their heads, how the engines were fairing during the last few seconds, how much the rocket was shaking and so forth. Each second lasted more than a page. It gave me an insight to how the use of different time aspects can give a story more meaning. About 15 pages later the rocket blasted off and was heading to the Moon. The rest of the story covered more feelings of solitude, and the thoughts of leaving loved ones back on Earth without knowing if they would make it back. They did make it to the Moon and back again, perhaps the characters grew during their trip, at least the readers (and listeners) got to know a lot about the characters and a lot of how a rocket may or may not work in real life.

Back to James Best. The theme for our fiction stories this time was about a historic period of our choice. At the time I was heavily addicted to Micropose's game Pirates. I used to play it, on my Commodore 64, as soon as I had some time over. For those of you who don't know what the game was about, it was a strategic/action game set in the Caribbean during the Pirate hey-days of 1560-1700. You could choose any 20-year period and it posed you with different levels of difficulty. For example the period of 1560-1600 (the longest of the periods) was difficult as there were almost only Spanish colonies at this time. You would have to keep friendly with Spanish and plunder the few non-Spanish colonies. Or you played it hard and attacked the Spanish colonies in the hopes of beating the odds. Another difficult era was the Pirate Sunset, 1680-1700. Here the climate of the colonies had changed drastically. Where pirates had previously been used to fight and plunder the enemy, they were now being hunted by powerful pirate hunting ships. The odds of surviving a fight with a pirate hunter was slim, making that time period incredibly difficult, not impossible, but difficult all the same.

The easiest time period was 1640-1660, at the height of the 30-year war. It was a bit of a free for all. Every colony was at war with each other, more or less. Getting titles and land was easy. The Spanish power was diminishing and the big and rich Spanish ports were easy targets. It was in to this era that I decided to write my story. It is one thing playing a 2 dimensional game, but to actually make a story out of it, well that is a whole different thing. I needed a protagonist worthy of the title of a story. James Best was born. He was a nobleman from England, that had decided to seek fame and fortune as a Privateer in the Caribbean. The story started off as a jolly escapade into piracy, plunder and a lot of rum flowing down the throats of all the members of the crew. When an attack on the colony Campeche turned sour, we saw a large amount of the crew imprisoned in the fortresses dungeon. James Best orders his ship, The Black Panther, to be sailed around to Belize, on the other side of the Peninsular and wait for him there, while he rescued the rest of the crew.

The break-in to the dungeon and the escape from it was described in detail, as was the flight across the jungle, which was infested with mosquitos, tribes of Indians and dangerous animals. Not many of the crew survived the trek across the jungle to Belize, but

James Best did.

The story ended in a bit of an odd way. I had wanted to make my own, and serious, version of Blackadder. The question of course was how would I get the Privateer James Best from the 1640's to the next period of time? I decided on alien abduction. I know, right! The story ended with James Best being transported onboard an alien spaceship. I later wrote two sequels to the story, one set in France during the revolution, and the next set in Germany during its union at the end of the 1800's. This produced more questions than I had answers for. I wanted to know more about James Best, who was he, why was he selected to travel through time. I then decided that there was more to him than all that. During one of my rewrites he became an immortal, rather than a time traveler. That of course brought about the questions of how he had become an immortal, where was he from, what historical events should he have experienced, affected, etc. James Best's story was starting to take form.

Over the years his story evolved and changed to suit plots that I came up with after a certain event had already happened. This way things that occur may not make any sense to the reader, and I will offer no proper explanation at the time. But in time an explanation will be offered that will make the reader go "aha! Now I see, now I know!" Or something to that effect.

The story that you are about to read is the first volume of The Adventures of James Best. Hope you enjoy it.

Timothy Frojd
Jersey Channel Islands
6th November 2017

Chapter 1

The smell was probably hideous, but I could no longer distinguish it, it had been my companion for far too long. I couldn't believe that there were still corpses lying around on the ground, slowly decomposing. There were no people left that could take care of corpses lying on the ground anymore. In fact, there weren't many around to take care of anything anymore. Those who were still around didn't care about anyone or anything other than themselves and what few belongings they still clinged to. Not to mention the mutants. The mutants were in abundance, especially in the ruins of what once had been magnificent and awe inspiring cities. I had tried to avoid the ruined cities for so long now. Something made me move towards this specific one. I couldn't explain the feeling, but it was as if something was pulling me there, calling for me. I couldn't ignore the feeling and turn around either, whatever it was that was pulling me there wouldn't let me turn around now. Only one way to go.

The hour was late, it was time to make camp for the night. Get some well-earned sleep. By mid-day tomorrow I should reach my goal.

I dreamt. I dreamt of the burning skies. The burning skies that had caused the scorched earth that we few survivors now shared and lived on. But in the dreams, there was also a huge ring of fire. Calling out to me. Calling me, telling me to come and touch it. Telling me I had to do it. Everything depended on me touching that ring of fire. Just before I managed to lay my hand on it, I awoke. I was sweating and had a strange, ominous feeling that something was terribly wrong. I packed up my few belongings and started out again towards the ruined city.

I had been right. By mid-day I saw the city on the horizon. I advanced with renewed vigour towards it. I soon saw the remains of a hanging bridge looming high up in the air. I was obviously walking on what had once been a river. Rivers were different to the oceans. Rivers were by no means as deep as the oceans. When I had been walking on what had once been the bottom of the ocean, I was further down than anyone had ever been before. Not many know this, but the bottom of the oceans are so deep that it would be the same distance from the surface to the bottom as it had been the distance from a plane to the surface. Now it made for a weird landscape covered in mountain ranges that would never have had been discovered or climbed, if not for the fire in the skies. If all the water in the world hadn't have boiled away. If not… if not…

Not long now and I would reach the bridge.

The silence that had become a norm for this world was suddenly broken by a loud noise that reminded me of a gun or rifle being fired. Something zinged past my head and I realised that it had been a gun or more likely a rifle that had been fired, and it had been fired at me. I stopped for a second and in that short second another bang was heard and I felt a burning sensation in my chest and then in my back. I had been hit. The bullet had hit me in the chest, and then gone out through my back. I screamed out, more in anger than in pain. Who was shooting at me? And where had he got hold of bullets? They were hard come by in these days. I was more angry that he was wasting bullets than I was of the fact that he had just shot me. I stood my ground and started, yet again, to advance towards the ruined city, not giving any heed to the mysterious gunman. I hadn't taken more than a few steps before I heard another loud bang, followed by two more in quick sequence. I felt the burning pain in my left thigh and then in my chest again. The third bullet hit my left frontal lobe and it managed to knock me to the ground. As usual when I had been shot, the pain was terrible. But I had to concentrate on the healing process, pushing out the bullets that hadn't passed through me and then healing those wounds as well. It was a process I had done many times before, and each time I did it was time consuming and just a tad painful. While I was lying on the ground, trying to heal myself, I heard shuffling feet approaching me. I opened one eye and looked. There were about a dozen mutants heading in my direction. Four of them were carrying rifles. The others were carrying axes, spades or other equally lethal tools. They walked slowly towards me. My healing process was far from finished, but I sensed that it might have to be postponed for a while. I saw one of the mutants, who was carrying a rifle, raise his weapon and with a loud bang noise he fired it at me. It hit me dead centre of my stomach. He fired again and the bullet burnt its way through my heart. The pain was a little more than an annoyance. I would have to do something before he splattered me all over the countryside. And I can tell you something, pulling yourself together after being blown to small bits like that is no easy task. I forced myself to stand up and reached for the handle of my sword that was hanging from my belt. I pushed a button on the handle and the blade came out with a swooshing noise. The mutants stopped in their tracks. They hadn't expected me to still be alive. I took advantage of their shock and started to cut them down with my sharp blade. The whole thing took little less than ten seconds. Their mutilated corpses lay strewn on the ground all around me. I continued my healing process as I retracted my blade again by a push of the same button and then hung it back on my belt.

I advanced yet again towards the ruins of the city, being ever more vigilant for more gunmen. Nothing happened. Maybe I had managed to scare the rest of them away with my resurrection. Soon I had entered the ruined city and I thought to myself that I did recognize it, although I couldn't place it at this very moment. I had been to so many cities in my life that they all became a blur of streets, buildings and bustling life. But nonetheless, this city did seem familiar. I walked up streets that were littered with decomposing corpses, garbage and other things that I didn't want to investigate any closer. The buildings sure had taken a beating from the fire in the skies, there wasn't much left of them worth calling a building. Although they were still standing, they looked as if they would crumble and fall at any time. I soon came to a large building and it still had some letters on it. I could read the following on it:

K NS M SEUM

Some kind of Museum obviously, but of no interest to me, I was being pulled to the left of the building towards a hill that led up to a few more buildings. But the buildings in themselves weren't interesting. It was what was in front of them that caught my eye. A large ring was placed as a monument on the ground. It was without a doubt the ring from my dream, and although it was not on fire here in the real world it was the same ring. I went up to it and touched it. Nothing happened. I touched it again. This time the same thing as before happened. I began to doubt if this really was the right ring, and thought to myself, why was I told in my dream to touch it but nothing happened when I did. I sat myself down on the bottom part of it and pondered my next move.

I had been sitting there for less than five minutes when I saw a small hatch on the inside part of the ring. I tried to pry it open but failed miserably. I tried and tried and then I tried some more, but nothing happened. I couldn't open it. Suddenly it swung open by itself. I was astonished. I looked inside and saw a button. I decided that the button was probably there for me to push, and that had been my whole reason for being here. My hand moved slowly towards the button, and then I withdrew it. What if this was all wrong? What if something bad would happen if I pushed the button? I let my hand wander towards the button again and then withdrew it once more. I gathered all my courage and will power and let my hand travel towards the button a third and final time. This time I pushed the button. At first nothing happened. Then all at once it was if reality took a step to the left.

Chapter 2

The ring exploded in fire. Or at least it seemed as if it exploded. What really happened was that the button had triggered something within the ring, I could see something that hadn't been there a few seconds ago, something that was only visible within the confines of the ring. It took me a few seconds to realise that I was probably looking at another world and not only that, I saw an army of short, muscular humanoids ready to come through the portal. Less than a second after my realisation the army advanced on me. I released my blade once again and started to hack away at the invaders. But there were way too many of them and soon they had inflicted too many wounds on me that I had difficulties keeping up with my healing. Finally, I fell to my knees and they overwhelmed me, clawing, punching and kicking at me. I did my best to try and defend myself. But my main priority was to conceal my sword. I retracted the blade and hid the handle in my coat. Then darkness came upon me.

When I awoke I found myself in some kind of cage. Correction, I found myself in a cage on wheels, being pulled by odd quadruped beasts. I tried hard to find my bearings. I couldn't have been out for very long, because we were not far from the remains of the hanging bridge, but it decreased in size for each minute that passed by. I forced myself to stop looking at the shrinking bridge and instead turn my attention to the invading force that was escorting me in my rolling prison. They were shorter than humans, very stocky built and their heads had a very low and flat top to them, it reminded me of how the Neanderthals had looked like but stockier, more – I don't know – rockier I guess, almost as if they were made of stone. Their clothes were not so different than those of early cave dwelling humans and the weapons that they carried reminded me of the clubs that early humans had wielded. I heard them grunt at each other, it sounded crude and guttural. I tried very hard to figure out what they were saying to each other. After listening for a while it started to sound as if they were talking English, although without all the vowels. It was the only thing that made sense of the sounds they were making. They didn't offer me many looks during our travel westward. It had to be westward. I looked behind me and saw the remains of the bridge that I had passed under mere hours ago, and the ruined city behind it. I suddenly, with clarity remembered what city it had once been. I had lived there.

It had been a city called Gothenburg. At least back in the days, before the fires in the skies had destroyed civilization as we know it.

When had I lived there? I tried to remember. It must have been during the 1980's. Yes, of course it was.

I had moved to Gothenburg, Sweden in order to find some peace and quiet. I was so tired of all the wars that I had been fighting in. Sweden was supposed to be a peaceful country. So, in the beginning of 1981, I found myself stepping off the plane in Landvetter, Gothenburg's airport. I caught a taxi into the city and found myself a small and cheap hotel. That night I slept better than I had done for a very long time. The next day I got up and looked for a job. I found one at a construction site, building the new and improved Gothenburg. A Gothenburg for the future, or at least that was what the slogans said back then anyway.

The years went by and I was enjoying my quite and peaceful life. Then came the day that stripped Sweden of its peace and innocence forever. I awoke one Saturday morning, put the TV on and was informed by an extra newscast that the Swedish prime minister had been gunned down outside a cinema, where he had been in just moments before, with his wife, watching, without knowing it, his last movie. Now some might argue, why the death of a prime minister should make such a big difference to a country and its inhabitants. Well for one thing, this specific prime minister was a good politician. At least as far as the people of Sweden were concerned. They loved him. I had come to admire him over the years that I had lived in the country. He seemed to be a good man and he was trying to make a difference. I had all but given up on ever being part of making a difference anymore. But at the event of his death, I once again pulled out my sword and decided it was time for me to contribute to this world once more. I went out to find the murderer. The trail was being covered up before I could trace the gunman. Someone very powerful was behind it. Officially his murder was never cleared up. But I found the murderer. At least I found out who was behind the murder, but alas I never managed to catch up with him.

After searching for years, I managed to track down the man who had wielded the deadly weapon. He was dying of some disease and I promised him an easy passing if he told me the whole truth behind the assassin. He did. Oh boy, did he ever. His story sounded so fantastic that I thought he was making it up at first. But he swore that it was all entirely true. The mastermind behind the assassin had been a crime lord based in London. He went by the name Mr E. I decided that it was time to return to England and more precise, London. It had been more than twenty years since I had been there.

I got a place to stay, then I went out hunting for Mr E.

It seemed as if Mr E was mixed up in all the crime that happened in London. There was nothing too small or too big for him to be part of. He truly was the lord of crime. He was also impossible to track down.

I decided that the best way of getting him, was to interfere as much as possible with his business. It paid off. In ways that I hadn't counted on. I had obviously annoyed him enough to force him to send out his top agents to try and have me wiped out. They started attacking me in waves. They had found out where I lived and forced me into hiding. I couldn't stay hidden for long, I had to try and get to Mr E before things got out of hand.

Then one day I met a formidable opponent. His punches and kicks sent me flying long distances, making me crash, painfully to the ground. He kept coming at me and when I managed to get in a punch or a kick, it felt as if I was hitting a wall. Then I realized that he wasn't human. He was a robot. Suddenly, he just left me alone. I didn't understand why. He could have broken me faster than I could heal myself.

A few months later, after fighting off loads of Mr E's agents, I had the surprise of my life. I was walking down a busy London street, when suddenly, I found myself standing face to face with myself. Well not myself of course, but an exact copy of me. He had hatred burning in his eyes. He smiled viciously at me and then before I knew what was going on, he had punched me. I found myself flying backwards and landing on a group of people. I got up and apologised to them. But before I could complete my apology my clone had attacked me again. He didn't seem to care about the people around him. When the people realised what was going on, they started screaming and running away. I got up, pulling out my sword and extracting the blade. He pulled out a similar sword, although his didn't seem to be of the retractable kind. He smiled at me, saying: "Didn't think that I would be THAT alike you, did you? Huh? Did you? Huh?" He continued smiling his vicious smile at me all the time. Our swords met with a loud clash. By then I could hear the sirens coming towards us in the not so far distance. The police would try to stop us, but I feared that my clone might be an immortal as well, and thus bullets wouldn't stop him. The question was of course; would I be able to? Our swords continued to clash loudly, all the time he was grinning his vicious grin. He was ruthless and relentless. He didn't care who got hurt or what got damaged. He was destroying cars, shop windows, lamp posts and more in his attempts to get me. The police cars screeched around the corner into the street where we were fighting. They came to a halt, and riot police poured out of the vehicles. They screamed their usual warning of "put down your weapons and surrender!" Well we weren't about to do that of course. I knew that my clone wouldn't comply, so that meant that I couldn't do it either. We continued to fight, despite the bullets that had started to hail towards us from the riot polices' guns. I felt the burning sensation each time a bullet found its way into my body. Some passed right through, but I sensed some of them were still in there. I put as much mental effort as I could afford, to locate the bullets and force them out of my body before the wounds healed and the nasty bullets would remain inside of me. That wouldn't be so nice. I would have to perform surgery on myself just to get them out. I didn't really fancy that. So far, I was getting all the bullets out of me. At the same time, I was still clashing swords with my mad clone. I could see that bullets had hit him as well, and found myself wondering if he also could do the same thing as me, or if he just let the bullets remain.

I dodged his sword and punched him in his stomach. He doubled over with the sudden pain. I then took my chance and gave him a hard uppercut that knocked him through a shop window. I jumped in through the broken window just in time to see him racing towards the shops exit. Had he had enough? I wasn't going to let him get away, he was my only lead to Mr E. I raced after him. We were inside a large multi-storey shopping centre and he headed towards the escalator, pushing his way past all the afternoon shoppers. I ran after him up the escalator, making apologies to everyone that he had pushed aside. When he reached the next floor, he picked up a showroom dummy and threw it towards me. He missed me but knocked out a few innocent shoppers instead. He continued up the next escalator and I had to hurry up if I wanted to catch up with him. He was ahead of me, but I wasn't going to give up. Once he reached the roof I would have him. And soon enough he did, and so did I. I confronted him standing on the edge of the roof, telling him to give up and tell me how to find Mr E. He snarled at me, turned his back towards me and made himself ready to jump. Pure madness, that was my thought at the time. But then I saw what his intentions had been. He hurled himself like a human missile towards the even taller building across the street. He crashed right through a window of the building. I was shocked at first, but found myself fast and decided to follow him, lest I'd lose him. I ran towards the edge and jumped. I could feel the air around me, and I remember thinking if this had been such a good idea after all. If I missed the building and fell to the street that would be very painful indeed. And the police were still down there. They would haul me away to prison before I could put myself back together again. I had no time for that. This was my chance to get to Mr E, and I wasn't going to let that chance slip through my *fingers. I didn't miss. I crashed through another window and landed badly on someone's computer. I got to my feet and saw my clone running towards the door. Everyone around me was in shock, and I could truly understand them. I ran after him again, hoping that soon it would all be over, and he wouldn't have anywhere else to run to. Yet again he headed for the roof. I increased my speed, ignoring the pain that was soaring through my knees after my bad landing. I soon reached the roof and found him yet again standing on the edge. But this time there wasn't any other building tall enough for him to reach with a jump. At least I hoped that that was the case. He turned his back towards me again, and I thought that this was it. He was going to jump. But that was not the case. He turned towards me again and snarled, showing his teeth. He looked towards the sky, as if waiting for something. And indeed, he was. I heard the familiar sound of a helicopter coming towards us. Was it the police? More likely it was agents of Mr E, coming to collect my clone and prepare him for round two. There was no way that I was going to let that happen. When the helicopter came closer, they let a rope ladder out and my clone grabbed hold of it and started a rapid climb. I jumped after him and grabbed a rung of the ladder just below him. He tried to kick me, but in the process he lost his balance and almost let go of it. He swore and snarled again. He continued to climb the ladder whilst the helicopter had started its ascent. We were now high above the city, flying north. At last, I would be taken to Mr E. Or at least that was what I hoped. Both my clone and the helicopter pilot were doing their best in trying to shake me off the ladder, but I wasn't letting it happen. Too much was at stake. I held on for dear life. Then it happened. An explosion so loud and intensive that the helicopter was instantly disintegrated and I found myself hurtling towards earth in a ball of fire. The sky was burning.*

Chapter 3

The wagon moved ever onwards, the ruined city of Gothenburg was now far behind us. The creatures moved with a speed that I hadn't thought was possible. Westwards, ever westwards. The sun was setting and we came to a stop. They set up camp for the night and put guards outside my mobile prison.

I didn't try to escape, I was too curious as to who these creatures were. If I escaped, I might never find out. I let sleep overcome me, and drifted slowly into the land of dreams.

I dreamt of nothing which was a change from all the dreams about that cursed portal.

I awakened during the night by the low conversation of my two guards. The more I listened to them, the more I was convinced that it was English, minus all the vowels. It sounded strange and I had to guess half the time as to what they were saying, but I was starting to get a grip on their language. They were talking about a special mission that was undertaken by some special taskforce. What that mission was all about, neither one of them knew. I managed to catch one of their names, it was Grgr if I wasn't much mistaken. I addressed him and they both turned towards me in surprise. The one that I thought was called Grgr looked at me as if he knew me. But that was of course impossible. The other guard started to poke me with his weapon. Grgr said something to the other guard and he stopped poking me. They had a heated discussion and it ended with the other guard leaving Grgr alone with me. Was this good or bad? Grgr looked at me again with the same look as before, as if he knew me. Suddenly he did something that surprised me. He unlocked my cage and motioned me to get out. Was this a trick? Was he letting me out so that he could kill me while escaping, becoming a hero amongst his people? Whatever his motives were, I wasn't going to let the chance slip through my fingers. I jumped out of the cage, gave Grgr a look of gratitude and then headed off. But the other guard had gone and raised the alarm and I suddenly had the entire army heading after me. I turned around and drew my sword and extended the blade. This time I was prepared so they wouldn't stand a chance. As I was fighting my way through a large group of creatures I caught sight of a giant of a man running towards us. He was carrying a large sledgehammer, which he lifted over his head as he closed in on the creatures and then he brought it down on them, spreading them to the left and to the right and in every other conceivable direction. Between the two of us, it didn't take long to wipe out the army of creatures. The gigantic man stood resting on his hammer, panting, trying to catch his breath after all the killing.

I withdrew my blade and hung the handle back on my belt. I went over to the man and extended my right hand. He didn't acknowledge it at first, he only stood hanging on his hammer, trying to breathe normally. He then turned his head to look at me through the mass of red hair that was hanging in front of his eyes. He hesitated for yet another few seconds before extending his gigantic hand and taking mine. I felt the pressure of his hand. A hand that surely could break stones if needed. He introduced himself as Jock. Jock Mac Tavish. He shook my hand up and down exactly three times then let it go. I told him my name. He told me that he was sorry that he had hesitated so long before shaking my hand, but he wasn't sure if I was a human or one of the many mutants that he had tangled with the past few years. But he had decided that I looked far too normal to be a mutant, and I sure wasn't one of the creatures that had invaded earth. I asked him if he had seen anymore of the creatures. He told me that he had run into some further east a few hours ago, and they had met with the same fate as the creatures that had held me prisoner. So where are you headed, I asked. He told me that he was on the way home after being on a small, pointless hunt for food. He had been tired of the few rabbits that inhabited the land where he lived. He was hungry for something bigger, something tastier. But alas there hadn't been anything at all to be found. I told him that the burning skies incident had killed off most of the animals and those few that survived had mutated, much in the same way that most of the humans had. He grunted. *Ye want some rabbit stew, Jimmy?* It sounded nice so I nodded. We headed westward to his home.

His home was built of stone and I got the feeling that I was in an old fairy tale, just waiting for someone to come in through the door, maybe the big bad wolf or even Snow white. Now Snow white wouldn't be too bad I mused. His home was decorated with a large table made from oak, two gigantic wooden chairs, an old black stove that was fuelled by earth that burnt giving off the needed heat for cooking, a gigantic bed and one comfy looking easy chair next to a fireplace.

Jock stood by the stove, stirring in a huge pot. He poured out the rabbit stew on two plates then handed me one of them. I ate heartily of the stew. It wasn't bad at all. But I could understand that he was tired of rabbits if that was the only thing that he ate. *So Jimmy, are ye gonna come with me then?* I was taken by surprise and that must have been reflected in my face, I stopped eating in the middle of a bite and I was aware that I had a piece of rabbit hanging out of my mouth. *What?* Was the only word that I could get out, mostly because I couldn't think of anything else to say, but also because of all the food in my mouth. *South, Jimmy. To Stonehenge.* I swallowed all the food I had in my mouth, let out a loud belch and tried to find something relevant to say. I finally said *but why Stonehenge?* Jock looked at me, shaking his head so that his massive, bushy hair swayed. *Haven't ye had the dreams Jimmy?* I shook my head. *What dreams Jock?* He started to tell me about a re-occurring dream that he had had for little more than a week. The dreams had been clear enough. He was to wait for a man that had been a prisoner, and then travel south to Stonehenge. I remembered the vivid dreams that I had had about the ring and they had turned out to be true. Devastatingly so. I told Jock about my dreams. He told me that if my dreams had been true, then his must surely be true. I remarked that as my dreams had resulted in the current situation with an invading army, then what guarantee did we have that his dreams wouldn't cause something even worse. He said that it could be worth going there to see what would happen once we reached Stonehenge, and anyway there were two of us now, so we should be able to handle any trouble that would come about. *But first we sleep, tomorrow we leave for Stonehenge.* He threw me some pillows and some covers and I camped out on the floor. It took me a while to fall asleep, but finally I drifted off into a dreamless sleep.

Early next morning we awoke and got ready for the trek south. Jock was carrying his big sledge hammer over his right shoulder. Other than that, he didn't bring anything. As we left his house, he turned to take one last look at it. *I doubt that I will ever see it again. I have a strange feeling that this trip will turn into an adventure, and that I won't survive it.* I tried to give him the old line of *No of course you won't die* but somehow it didn't sound as good as it used to do in the movies. *Jimmy, there is one thing that I need to tell ye about the path that we will be taking. It is riddled with mutants. They don't like normal humans so we are likely to have to fight our way south.* I nodded silently, whilst thumbing the handle of my sword.

We headed south along a small path, leaving the house behind us. We walked in absolute silence for the better part of an hour, then Jock broke the silence by starting to whistle. Utter surprise took me. It seemed out of character for him to whistle. But it sounded good and it was a melody that I knew. Although I couldn't for the world remember the name of the song or what the group was called, but I remembered that they were Scottish twins. I joined in on the whistling for a while. The sun was shining and it was nice and warm. I was wondering when something would go wrong, it usually did when things were looking this good. As nothing can be this good for too long. An unwritten law I suppose. Murphy's law or something equally stupid.

Jock suddenly stopped whistling and motioned me to silence. He was looking from his right to his left and back again. *Mutants!* He said. I drew out my sword handle and extended the blade. No sooner had I done that, the first mutants came into sight, running towards us, wielding makeshift weapons. Soon the hills around us were swarming with mutants, all armed to the teeth.

Ten minutes later the battle was over, although it felt longer than that. The dead mutants were strewn around on the ground. I wiped my blade clean and then retracted it. Jock cleaned his hammer head and then swung it up on to his shoulder again without a word. We continued our journey south in silence. One thing you could say about Jock, was that he wasn't one for saying much. But then he surprised me again. *Jimmy, do you know what I was before the burning skies?* Taken by surprise, yet again, it took me awhile before I answered him with a *No.* He was silent for a few minutes and then told me. *I used to work as an insurance agent for a huge insurance company. We would insure almost anything against almost anything. Ironic isn't it that nothing was insured against what happened that fateful day.* I nodded silently. *I had a nice house, a lovely wife, two great kids, two cars, membership at St Andrews golf club, a summer house in the south of Spain, a nice sailing boat, and about £300,000 tucked away in my bank. What good is it all now? My wife and children died due to the burning skies. I survived! For what? Why? Why me? Why didn't I die alongside my wife and children? Why did I have to witness their deaths?* I swallowed, didn't know what to say to console this giant of a man, whose tears were running down his cheeks. *All that I had, all that I ever loved, gone! Do ye know what that is like Jimmy? Do ye?* I did, of course I did, all too many times had loved ones been taken from me by their old age, while I kept on living, never aging and never changing. But how could I tell him this without sounding like a liar, or someone who is pulling his leg, making fun of his sorrow. So, I thought it best not to say anything at all. His tears were running down his cheeks without control now. He stopped and sat down on the ground, putting his gigantic hands over his face. He then started to sob loudly. I sat myself down next to him, not sure what to do. I tried to put my hand on his shoulder, hoping that he would take it as a sign of me wanting to give him my support in his sadness. He continued sobbing loudly for some time. Then finally it seemed as if there were no more tears left in him. He looked up at me, with red eyes. His lips were trembling as he began to speak to me. *I'm sorry Jimmy, didn't mean to let things get out of control like this. It is just... It is just... I haven't had a chance to tell anyone about this until now, as ye are the first person, well non-mutant anyway, that I have met since the fire in the skies. I've kept it bottled up in me all this time, and when I started telling ye about it, I suddenly realised that it was all like a saucepan on the stove that is set to boil over and there isn't anything that ye can do about it. Nothing at all! I just boiled over. That is it. That is all. End of story. End of it! No more!* I wanted to tell him that I knew how he felt, but I found it difficult without telling him that I was an immortal. We got up and continued our walk south, in silence once again.

After a few hours of walking in silence, Jock started talking with me, about this, that and the other. It seemed as if he was starting to feel better after his catharsis earlier. I felt glad for his sake. We walked and talked, and fought and killed mutants and felt no worse for it.

We didn't feel like much would surprise us, but what we saw when we came to the top of a hill defied all belief.

In the not so far distance was a small forest. But how could that be. All trees and their seeds had been destroyed due to the fire in the skies. But, there, in front of our very eyes was evidence that proved us wrong. We looked at each other in amazement. I wondered if we should go down and investigate it or avoid it. Jock thought that it couldn't do any harm to go into it. So, we descended the hill and the forest seemed to grow as we got closer to it. Before long we were standing in the shade of the trees. I took a deep breath of the air in the forest. The smell in there was something I hadn't felt in a long time. It felt good. It felt invigorating. Jock was doing likewise. I went over to a tree and felt it, it felt real enough. But how could this be? This forest shouldn't be here. But I was glad that it was. That meant that nature was trying to return from being scorched, and that was a very good thing. We continued deeper into the forest, where it was getting darker because of the dense crowns of the trees.

Chapter 4

We had been walking for almost half an hour in the semi-darkness of the forest when we saw a light up ahead. It was a small clearing, and the sun was shining down on it. But it wasn't the clearing that was the fascinating thing. It was the small cottage standing in the centre of the clearing. Once again, we looked at each other in amazement. Would it be safe to enter the cottage? Once again, I thought of old fairy tales where people went into strange cottages in the middle of woods and would never came out again, because in the cottage there would live an evil witch or a nasty troll that ate humans and grinded their bones. But then again, it could be all innocent like Snow white living there. And that wouldn't be too bad really. While I had been standing around thinking about fairytales and Snow white, Jock had ventured up to the door of the cottage and opened the door.

Before I could react, Jock had entered the cottage and disappeared. My legs felt as if they were made from lead as I tried to follow Jock. I needed to get my act together. I concentrated and finally managed to make my legs move in an ordinary speed towards the cottage. As I got closer I noticed there was a sign hanging over the door. The reason I had missed this from a distance was that I was seeing it from the side. I rounded it and looked at what was on it. *The Green Hornet* was its name. A pang of remembrance hit me smack in the middle of my stomach. The reason for this was that on the sign was also an old plane, a Hurricane. I felt my skin ripple. It had been a very, very long time since I had seen a Hurricane. Something like 70 odd years. With a lump of ice in the pit of my stomach I reached for the door handle and turned the knob. I pushed the door inwards and the smell of a roasted pig hit my nostrils. It wasn't very light inside the tavern, so my eyes were having some problems adjusting to the semi-darkness of the room. I looked over to the right and saw a large fireplace. A whole pig was roasting over it on a large spit. I looked straight into the room and saw a small bar in the far end of the room, there were glasses of ale on it and behind the bar I could see some bottles and barrels that I guessed contained ale. I turned and looked to my left and saw Jock sitting at a large wooden table being served by a youngish looking normal human. I walked over to them and slid myself down on the bench opposite Jock. I smiled and turned my face towards the young man that was taking Jocks order. If I had experienced a pang of remembrance from seeing the Hurricane on the sign outside, it was nothing like the full wallop that I felt now. I knew the man that was taking my order, although I had thought him long dead. My jaw dropped to the table. I don't think he recognised me at first, but after what seemed like an eternity, he stopped talking and took a closer look at me. His jaw dropped as well. We both stared at each other with our jaws hanging closer to the ground than what was good for us, there were after all loads of insects about. He was the first one to compose himself. His jaw slowly returned to its normal position again. I could see and hear him swallow loudly. He cleared his throat and then he spoke again. *If I didn't know better, I would say that you are Captain Best. But that cannot be. You died many years ago.* I finally let my jaw return to normal again. I had been right. It was him. Impossible but true. *And if I didn't know better I would think that you were Major White.* His jaw dropped again, but soon returned to where it should be. His face quickly turned into a smile. *James!* I jumped out from the bench that I was sitting on, embraced him, and took a step back to take a better look at him. *William? How can this be? I was so sure that you died during our attack on Rommel's fortress.* William looked at me and his smile widened, he nodded slowly. *And I believed you dead too. But obviously, we are both blessed, or cursed, with long lives.* I suddenly remembered that Jock was sitting at the table. I turned to look at him. I must have looked as guilty as a boy caught with his hand in the cookie jar, because Jock smiled and said *No need to worry Jimmy, I've known all the time that ye were an immortal, the person in my dream told me as much, and now I am absolutely sure that you are the one mentioned to me in it.* Yet again Jock had surprised me, he was truly a man of many surprises.

William told us that he was just going to get us some food and some ale and then he would join us for a chat. He was curious as to what had happened after the attack on the fortress all those years ago.

It didn't take long before he returned carrying three plates containing nice juicy pieces of pork and lovely golden potatoes. He returned to the bar and grabbed three jugs of ale and then brought them over to us. *Please tell me what happened to you, James. I am curious. Then I will tell you what happened to me.* I took a piece of pork and chewed on it for a few seconds. It was truly juicy and nice. However, it did leave me wondering as to where it had come from, seeing as almost all animals had died out all those years ago, and to my knowledge, no pigs had survived, in fact no large animals at all had survived. Rats, rabbits, and other smaller ones had of course, but anything larger than a small cat had perished. So where had it come from? But that was a question to be asked and hopefully answered later. First, I would tell William and Jock what had happened to me after the fateful attack on Rommel's fortress.

I will start my tale on the morning of the attack. Our orders had come five days previously and the planes that we were going to use had arrived the day before. They were small planes that had been used during the Great war almost twenty years earlier. They were packed with explosives and we were going to fly them straight into the fortress past the gigantic cannons and blow the entire concrete monster to smithereens.

Seven of us were going to fly the small bi-planes. Two of our squadron were going to act as an escort to make sure that we had a fighting chance at reaching the fortress. We were all very nervous, we all knew that this would be the end of us and of Hornet Squadron. The two pilots who were going to fly the Hurricanes that would escort us had been given the orders to make sure that we would be mentioned in the history books, so they had better survive to write it all down.

We all said our goodbyes and then went to our allocated aircraft. I climbed up into the cockpit of the ancient Camel and started it up.

The others did likewise. I looked over to the Camel in which my friend and Commander sat. William did thumbs up and waved to me. I reluctantly did the same. I knew that I would survive, what ever happened, but none of the others would have that same chance. William gave us the all clear sign and we let our planes taxi out on the makeshift runway. A few seconds later we were all speeding down the runway and very soon we were airborne. Then we headed north. Towards the fortress. Towards death.

The sun hadn't started to rise yet as our planes made their way across the desert. Somewhere in the distance the fortress was waiting for us. The fortress had six gigantic cannons, three pointing inland and three pointing towards the open sea. On the fortress roof were about thirty anti aircraft guns, placed in strategic positions. Any ship trying to get the fortress from the sea would be destroyed by the big cannons, or by one of the twelve smaller cannons that were mobile. Anyone trying to reach the fortress from land would be blown to bits by the minefield that surrounded it. If that wasn't enough the whole area was littered with small bunkers that had both anti aircraft guns and other weapons to be able to handle any attacks from any direction. And as if that wasn't enough, a nearby airfield supplied air support from the Luftwaffe. If there ever had been a suicide mission, this was it. To sum things up folks, it was impossible to attack the fortress from land, sea or air. But we were going to give it our best shot. In order to succeed we would have to fly our planes into the opening of the fortress where the cannons pointing towards land were. Thus, giving us a chance at stopping our planes as close to the cannons that were pointing towards the ocean. If these cannons could be destroyed, then the British Royal Navy could start their attack and destroy the rest of the fortress. It all depended on if we were successful or not.

Just as the sun started to rise, we saw the lethal gauntlet that awaited us. And there in the distance like a slumbering giant; the fortress. The Germans had been caught by surprise, not expecting an attack so early. But I must give them credit for getting organised so quickly. Soon the flak started. We tried to dodge the *flak as much as we could, but it seemed a lost cause. We lost Simpson and Wallis within the first few minutes. We still pushed on. There was no use in turning back. We all knew what was at stake if we failed. Suddenly an ear-shattering sound hit my ears. Something huge flew past us and ripped poor Jones and his plane to pieces. It was a projectile from one of the huge cannons from the fortress. The Germans were giving their everything to stop us. That was when the Messerschmitts turned up and started to fire upon us. Lewis and Clarke who were flying the Hurricanes gave us as much support that we needed to get on with our mission. But it still seemed as if we were all doomed as even Petrovicz got blown up, leaving me, William and Loomis to try and finish off the fortress. We were very close to the fortress and Loomis pulled ahead of us but misjudged the opening and hit the wall instead, turning his plane in to a fireball. I saw William land his plane and a few seconds later I joined him. We got out of the planes as fast as we could and started to light all the fuses. We had about sixty separate fuses to light. This was so that the Germans wouldn't be able to defuse the explosives before the time had run out. The Germans were running up behind us and shouting at us to give up. They didn't dare shoot, because my guess was that they knew very well what our planes were packing. Once I had set off all my fuses I turned around to face them. William had done likewise. We stood facing the barrels of a dozen German machineguns. The owners of the guns didn't look older than teenagers. They were as scared as I reckon anyone should be in the knowledge that they were facing certain death.*

That was when I heard the explosives go off. It was an amazing loud sound. I felt myself being pushed forward towards the Germans and at the same time I felt the concrete ceiling fall on me and then everything went dark.

The next thing I knew was waking up in complete darkness and digging myself out of the concrete mess. My wounds had managed to heal while I was unconscious, but I was covered in blood and dust. I had to get out of there as fast as possible, but then I heard the booming from the Navy. Once more the ceiling came tumbling down around me. I remained conscious and commenced in trying to claw my way out of the rubble. I finally managed to get clear of it all and found myself tumbling in a disorderly fashion towards the ground. I hit the sand with a heavy thud and got to my feet as fast as I could. German soldiers were running towards me and the only weapon I had on me was my sword. I pulled out the handle and extracted the blade. Then I swung into action against the Krauts. I felt bullets from their machineguns tear into my flesh as I fended off their attack. Finally, there were no more Germans left to fight and I sunk to the ground, retracted the blade and hung the handle back on my belt, I then collapsed on the ground and later found myself waking up in a hospital bed. That, my friends, is what happened to me on that fateful day so many years ago. Now William please tell me what happened to you and what have you been up to since the war?

William cleared his throat and was just about to speak when the door opened and a gang of mutants entered the room. I reached for my sword and Jock reached for his hammer, but we were both stopped by William.

Chapter 5

Both Jock and I gave William disapproving looks. *They are my customers, my guests.* We must have looked truly shocked because William got a bit embarrassed and then he explained that the local mutants were as much humans as the rest of us and that they were just as hungry as anyone normal and therefore had just as much right to eat as anyone else. It was my turn to feel ashamed. But I found myself quickly. Then an idea struck me. It was as strange an idea as ideas could be. But all the same, it might just work, and be beneficial as well.

I got up from the table and walked over to the table where the mutants were gathered. As soon as I approached, they jumped up and pulled out their makeshift weapons. I raised my empty hands and tried to pacify them. *Now please listen, I have a request to make of you, and I hope that you will hear me out before you decide to slice and dice me with your sharp and pointy weapons.* The mutants looked at each other for a long time, then they huddled together and whispered words that I couldn't hear. Finally, they stopped whispering, broke up the huddle and faced me, this time without the weapons. One of the mutants started to speak. He was pretty ugly, his face looked as if it had melted and his nose was closer to his chin than to his eyes. His eyes, or should I say eye, as in singular, had crept higher up his forehead which made him look more like a Cyclops from the mythology of ancient Greece.

Just because we look like monsters doesn't make us monsters. His words sounded a bit distorted, but considering his mouth looked all wrinkled and pretty tiny, it was no wonder.

I shook my head. *No I don't want to treat you as monsters either. I know you only want to survive just like everyone else does.*

He nodded slowly and extended his right hand to me. It looked as melted and deformed as his face. I took it and shook it. It felt truly strange, more like an elbow or a knee than a hand.

My name used to be Kirby, but now it isn't. He paused for a bit and I thought that I caught a glimpse of a tear falling from his eye. *Now I am mostly known as Polyphemus. Tell me what it is that you request of us. But don't expect too much of us. First of all, we are very hungry. Second, we don't really like or trust norms, mainly because norms don't like or trust us. So, with that said, what is it you want of us?*

This was going to call for some proper tact if it was going to pan out.

Polyphemus, what do you know of the invasion? Both Polyphemus and his friends looked at each other and seemed uneasy at the mention of the invasion. *All I know is that the creatures are not from here, they look more different than we do and they kill.* I nodded. *What I would like you to do for me, well not only for me, but for every living being on Earth, is to try and gather as many people like you as possible and start fighting back. Maybe this way we can be rid of the invaders and the norms will change their views about you.*

People will like us? He mused. *Hah! Norms liking us, norms trusting us. That will be the day. But still, your words do hold some truth in them. If these invaders are left alone to do whatever they want here, then Earth and all its inhabitants are surely doomed. Yes, I will try and unite my kind of people. Though I don't believe that I will have much luck in doing so. Becoming... different has made most people afraid of others, not only norms, but people that are different too. So, you see, your request might not be such an easy or small one. But nonetheless, I will give it my best and hope you won't be disappointed in what I can achieve. Though I know that I will be disappointed once it is all over and the norms still won't accept us.* His eye looked me straight into my eyes and I felt almost like a mental push as he did so. *William bring us some food and ale, we are now in a hurry. We have a task to do, and not much time to do it in.* He sat down, his friends did likewise. He didn't look at me again, so I slowly turned around and walked over to my table. William was already on his way to the kitchen to get them food. Jock looked at me and shook his head. *Ye ken Jimmy, they be right. Even if they do drive out the invaders, no norms will ever trust someone different like them. Even if you and I and young William will, there are those who fear what they don't know or understand.*

Of course, I knew all this and it was a chance that I was willing to take. Playing with others lives again. Would I ever learn? The end justifies the means. It just had to. They had to play their part in this as did the rest of us. And what would await us at Stonehenge? And why wasn't I dreaming about it? A million questions that still lingered and may one day be answered. But as for now? Eat, drink and be merry, for tomorrow we all might die. Even me? When will that day come, when I can be laid to rest forever and not have to walk the Earth, witnessing my friends and loved ones grow old and die.

But now I had met up with an old friend, who turned out to be like me, so maybe immortality could be a little more bearable now that I knew that I wasn't alone.

Stonehenge may linger in my thoughts, but first we will spend the night here in William's tavern. And maybe tomorrow he can be persuaded to follow us to our destination.

While I had been letting my thoughts carry me off to la la land, Polyphemus and his friends had finished their meal, drunk their ale and were on their way out through the door. Before he left the tavern, he turned towards me and gave me a final look. Then he was gone. Was he going to do as I had bid? No one could know for certain. But he did seem like an honest person. I decided to trust him. Our paths were sure to cross again someday.

William cleared our tables and then asked us if we needed rooms for the night, as it was starting to get dark outside. Both I and Jock thought it sounded like a good idea. So, he led us upstairs where the rooms were.

That night I slept in a bed for the first time in a long time and possibly the very last time too, I knew that it would be a very long time before I would get a chance to do it again.

Chapter 6

When we awoke the next morning, William had already made us our breakfast. The lovely smell of bacon, eggs, toast and tea reached my nostrils. How long had it been since I had smelt something so lovely? I went downstairs and sat myself at the table and started to fork in the food. A few moments later Jock came downstairs, rubbing his belly, saying *Mmm that smells really good. Better than rabbit stew.* He then gave a little laugh and I joined him in it. It felt good to laugh, it was always so long periods of time between the opportunities to laugh. It felt liberating, it felt good. Jock sat down and started to eat the bacon and eggs. William came in and joined us. I proceeded to ask him if he wanted to come with us to Stonehenge. I wasn't really prepared to hear what he had to say. *James, this is my home, I run this lovely little tavern and the people in these parts need me, my food and my ale. They need me to survive, and to make their lives a little happier. If not for that, I would not have come anyway. I have left my adventuring days behind me, accepted that I am not like you, I am not a warrior, I am at the best of times a scientist of many sciences and times like this I am an innkeeper, a supplier of food and drink. No James, I think this one is for you and for Jock, maybe for Polyphemus and his friends too. But not for me.*
I was so desperate for an immortal friend, that I wasn't willing to take no for an answer. We discussed the whys and the why-nots for what seemed like ages, until I finally realised that, no matter what I said, William wasn't going to change his mind.

William made us packed lunches for our travel south. They wouldn't last for more than three days, but by then we should have arrived at our destination.

We were out of the woods, literally. A few hours had seen us go through the dark woods and out into the scorched Earth again. It soon seemed as if we had been dreaming. But it was enough to turn around and see a glimpse of the forest to be assured that it hadn't been a dream.

We stopped to have something to eat and I was overjoyed that it was ham and cheese sandwiches, my favourite. After we had eaten our sandwiches, we continued our journey.

We passed many ruined towns and villages on our way. But what gave us the biggest shock was when after a whole day of walking we reached what was left of London, which is to say more than we had expected. London had been where I was when everything went wrong, when the skies had started to burn. But I didn't remain for long in London in the wake of the catastrophe, I fled into the countryside and continued forever away from that city. Not really knowing why I was fleeing or where I was heading, but I continued forever away from London. Today was the first time I had been back since that terrible day.

We were on a small hill just north of the city. What we could see was that most of the buildings were still more or less intact, but in ruins just the same.

Jock pointed at something, but I had difficulties in seeing what it was that he was pointing at, then I saw movement. Hundreds, maybe even thousands of figures were scuttling around on the streets. *Mutants most likely.* Jock said, in a matter of fact sort of way. I agreed with him that they were probably mutants. And that we should probably avoid London for the good of everyone. Hopefully Polyphemus would reach here and not meet with any trouble from the local mutants. But until then, we would do best to avoid any more encounters with them. We didn't want to risk killing any more potential allies.

We circumvented London as well as we could and didn't encounter any mutants on the way. Which I felt was a good thing. I had, thanks to Polyphemus, started to see them in a different light. Not just because I wanted them as allies, but because he had proven to me that they were not really any different from us.

Then in the early hours of the next day, we reached our destination. Stonehenge stood as firm, beautiful and mysterious as it always had done. The catastrophe hadn't touched it.

What were we doing here? I hoped that Jock had the answer to that. I turned towards the giant and saw that his eyes were closed, his lips moving silently, as if he was talking with someone that was invisible to me. After a few minutes of mumbling silently, his eyes opened. He looked straight towards the stones, took a firm grip on the hilt of his sledge hammer and strode over to the formation. He lifted the hammer and let it fall down on one of the stones. A sound like an explosion could be heard and both me and Jock were flung backwards. I got to my feet and helped Jock up. *What have you done?* He looked at me with fear in his eyes. *I ken not Jimmy, it feels as if I have awoken from a very long and terrifying dream. The hooded figure spoke to me, lead me here, told me to destroy that stone. Now the hooded figure is out of my mind and I don't ken what is happening.*
Jock looked truly terrified.

Jock was right of course, the hooded figure was no longer in his dreams. He was standing in front of us. It was as if no light could penetrate the darkness around him. The hooded figure laughed a truly evil laugh and then moved swiftly towards us. I averted my eyes as he drew near.
Get up Black Panther, and stop cowering on the ground like that. We have work to do and not much time left to do it in.
I looked up at the hooded figure and managed to see through the darkness that surrounded him. And I recognised him.
Merlin?
He stretched out his right hand, offering it to me to help me up from my position on the ground.
Aye! It is I, Merlin. Now let us not tarry. Arthur must be awakened and the knights must return to their former glory.
Merlin turned from us and walked in to the centre of Stonehenge and started to mutter some strange incantation, it soon rose in

volume and I could hear that he was calling out the names of all the knights of the round table.

Come here Sir Aglovale, Come here Sir Agravaine, Return to me Sir Anselm, Come here SirBediver…

And so he carried on for what seemed like ages until he suddenly went all silent. He turned towards us once again and strode over.

The deed is done, no way back now. Now we head for Glastonbury Tor to wake Arthur from his deep sleep. Onwards to Glastonbury! The others will meet us there.

And then he strode off, away from us, expecting us to be able to keep the same speed.

It took us a few moments to realise that we were going to be left behind if we didn't get in to gear and follow Merlin to Glastonbury. We had to run to keep up with him.

A few hours later we reached Glastonbury and I could see that some of the knights had already arrived there. I walked over to them and was overwhelmed by memories and emotions that I had considered long gone. Sir Tristan came over to me and embraced me.

When he let me go I could see tears streaming down his face.

Lancelot! You made it too. I am so glad to see you. You most of all, but gladder still will I be when Arthur once again walks amongst us.

Same old Tristan, I just hope that all the internal conflicts amongst the knights were gone and that we would all be able to become organised and defeat these invaders.

Merlin had, in the mean time, gone over to the Tor and stood chanting next to it. There was a loud booming sound and a bolt of lightning struck the Tor. It split in two pieces and they rolled down the hill. In the smoke that had emanated when the lightning struck, the shape of a tall man could be seen. The eyes of every knight, and anyone else that was fortunate to be there that day, turned towards the hill and the figure of the man. The smoke cleared and it was now obvious who was standing ever so regal on top of the hill. In unison, the knights started shouting *Arthur! Arthur! Arthur!*

Repeatedly. I joined in, after all, I had once been a knight.

Arthur stood and surveyed what lay beneath him and then after a long moment of silence from him, whilst we all were calling out his name, he spoke and we all went silent.

Knights! Britons! Brothers! Stand fast and listen to me. Merlin has filled me in on what is going on here. Not only is Britain threatened by an invading force, but this time the entire world is in grave danger. We are to put a stop to this threat! By God and the Grail, we will fight and we will win!

To this retort every knight, again, erupted in a hearty *Arthur! Arthur! Arthur!* Again repeatedly. This time I didn't join in. For some reason, it reminded me of something completely different, something that had happened more than 70 years ago and was not a very positive event.

Arthur put up his hands and motioned the knights to be silent once again.

I understand that there is a portal to the invaders world somewhere to the north east. I propose that we head for that portal and destroy it. That way they won't be able to get any reinforcements and we can defeat the remainder of their armies without any problem.

At this the knights erupted once again, chanting Arthurs name repeatedly.

Once again Arthur motioned silence.

Let's move out!

At that point, Arthur pointed to the north east and all the knights turned in that direction and started moving.

Jock approached me.

Jimmy, do ye have a bad feeling about this?

I nodded slowly, but if all this was a bad idea, it didn't really matter now. The die was cast, no turning back. For the moment, we needed to defeat the invaders and we were going to need all the help we could get. I started to move in the same direction as the knights. A marching song soon spread amongst the knights and soon I found myself singing along with the rest. We were going to war, and this time I wasn't so sure about Arthur as I had been all those centuries ago.

Chapter 7

We made camp that night not far from where Hadrian's Wall had been once upon a time, but now there wasn't much left of it.
I was getting ready to sleep when Arthur entered my tent.
Lance! It has been too long.
I nodded. It had been long, but perhaps not long enough. We hadn't exactly parted as good friends. But after Arthur's supposed death, I grieved his passing as did we all. But now he was back again. Had he changed? Had things changed between us?
A very long time Arthur. But I must ask you something. How are things between us?
Arthur looked confused.
What do you mean Lance?
I paused.
Well… You know… Your lady.
I regretted saying it even as I left my lips. I was waiting for his usual temper to erupt and for him to strike out at me. But nothing happened. He wasn't even angry.
Oh, come now Lance. That was almost 2000 years ago. I loved her and you loved her. She loved me, but loved you more. It is hardly something I can hold a grudge against you for. I have long since forgiven you… Brother!
He then came over to me and embraced me. It felt strange and I wasn't sure about it at all. Maybe it was just me. Maybe it was guilt. My guilt that had haunted me for decades afterwards, but had slowly diminished into oblivion over the centuries that passed by. But now the memories where back and so was my guilt. Was that the reason I felt suspicious towards Arthur?
Arthur let me go.
Tell me a story Lance. Please, I beg of you. The night is long and I can't sleep on the eve of a battle. Tell me a story.
I was surprised at this. What did he want to hear? Did he want me to justify my feelings towards Guinevere? Or was he truly a pre-battle insomniac?
What would you like to hear?
Arthur thought for a moment.

I think I would like to hear what happened to you after my death. Oh, you won't have to tell me everything up until this morning, but tell me as much as you can until the sun rises and we have to move out.

I couldn't believe what I was hearing. He wanted me to talk all through the night. After a few moments of thinking it through, I decided to give him what he wanted.

Ok! I'll tell you what happened to me after I heard about your death. I think you better sit down. And me too I think.

We sat down on the ground and I started telling him my story.

Things were breaking down everywhere. Mordred's knights were everywhere and they were winning. Your knights were in disarray, running away from the battle. The word reached us that you were dead and then suddenly there seemed like little point to stay and fight a losing battle. I left! Not only the battle field, but I left Britain too. It seemed the only way forward for me. I got a boat that took me to the land of the Franks. Tribes of barbarians were ravaging through Europe and there wasn't much space for me to rest. I fought my way east. Taking work as a mercenary for kings and lords in all too many places, all too many battles and against all too many barbarian hordes. I soon grew tired of it all and headed east. Eastwards to a country that would be known as China, if it wasn't already. It was a strange country with people who were slow to anger, but if they got angry, well you'd better stay out of their way. They could fight a tiger with their bare hands. But I didn't stop my travels in this remarkable country. There was something calling out to me. I wasn't aware as to who or what it was that was calling me, but I felt compelled to get a boat and head for the islands of the Nippon-Koku. The voyage cross the sea was rough but once we reached the shores of Nippon-Koku the sun was shining and I made my way inland, following the pull of whatever or whoever was calling out to me.

I walked for what seemed an eternity when suddenly I came upon the great mountain of Fuji that I could espy in the far distance. I was being pulled towards this towering cone shaped mountain and

*had no idea why. I reached a great lake and rounded it. As I was
coming around the lake I saw a building surrounded by a wall. I
walked up to the wall and followed it around until I came upon a
large wooden gate. Without being able to control myself, I knocked
hard on the large gate. For several minutes, nothing happened, so
I found myself knocking on the gate again. This time it didn't take
long before I heard a noise behind the gate and it swung open
silently. In front of me stood a small man, dressed in black. He
looked at me for the longest time and then gestured with his hand
for me to follow him. I followed the small man into the compound.
We were heading towards the building I had seen earlier, before
reaching the wall. As we drew closer to the building I saw a man
sitting on the porch. He had long white hair and his features
differed slightly from the small man and from any other person I
had encountered in Nippon-Koku. When I came to the foot of the
stairs leading up to the porch of the building, the man with the
long white hair stood up and looked at me. He was extremely tall,
at least a full head taller than me. He motioned to the small man
that had lead me here and the small man left. The man with the
white hair came down from the porch and circled me silently. So
far no one had said a word since I arrived. He circled me several
times and I was feeling very uneasy. Finally, he stopped in front of
me, bowed his head and spoke: "At last you have come, I was
afraid that you wouldn't, and if you had it wouldn't have been
you."
That was as cryptic as it could get. I had no idea what he was
talking about. I tried to ask him what he meant, but as soon as I
opened my mouth, he motioned me to silence.
"Time it is for training!" I couldn't believe it. Training? What kind
of training did he mean? He started to walk away from me and
then suddenly he turned towards me and ran as fast as the wind at
me and before I had time to react he had knocked me to the
ground. As I hit the ground I let a loud groan escape my lips. I was
dazed and confused. I tried to focus and saw the man standing,
towering over me, shaking his head. "Not good!" I managed to get
to my feet. But no sooner had I got up than the man moved without*

moving, if that makes any sense. It was the only way I can describe what I saw. It didn't appear as if he moved, but he still managed to knock me back to the ground again. This happened repeatedly. Each time I managed to get back I was knocked to the ground. Finally, I had had enough and cried out for mercy. The man turned his back on me and walked away. I took my chance and ran after him, ready to jump on to his back and wrestle him to the ground. But by the time I was in the air and should have landed on top of him, he wasn't there, which I realised when I landed hard on the ground. I turned over on to my back and saw the man standing, towering over me again. "Maybe we can make something of you even though you are totally useless in close combat." He then turned his back on me again and walked away. This time I didn't attempt to attack him. I just remained on the ground, dazed and out of focus.

I was suddenly aware that I wasn't alone. I looked around and saw the small man that had let me in through the gate, what seemed like ages ago, but hadn't been more than half an hour ago. He motioned to me to come with him. I suspected it was for more beating, but I followed him anyway. He showed me to a small hut close to the main building, he gestured to me to go inside, I complied with his wish. Inside the hut, I found a small bed, which looked really inviting. I got on the bed and within seconds I was fast asleep.

The next morning the small man woke me up and he took me outside to the porch of the main building, where the man with the white hair was sitting, just like the day before. Once I reached the porch, the small man bowed and then left me with the white-haired man. I prepared myself for another beating, but the man sat still and silent on the porch. I started to feel uneasy again. What were his intentions? What was my role in all of this?

The man remained still and silent for what seemed like ages. Then suddenly he got up and came down the porch and walked up to me. "Lesson two!"

Before I had a chance to react to his words, I found myself being knocked to the ground. I needed to think of something to do to be *able to remain standing. I squinted my eyes and as I did, I managed to actually see the man move. I was so surprised by this that I let his fist make contact with me and I fell once again to the ground. I got up and this time I was more prepared. I squinted again and this time when his fist was moving towards me I managed to avoid it by moving in the opposite direction. I was elated, so much that I didn't notice that the mans attack was far from over. He followed the hit with a leg sweep. Once again, I hit the ground. I got up and squinted. This time I would be prepared for everything. And I was successful for at least three minutes. But he finally overcame me as I couldn't maintain my squint anymore. He stood towering over me again. I was expecting him to turn and walk away, but instead he reached out his hand and helped me to my feet. Once on my feet, I expected him to attack again, but he didn't. I looked at him in amazement and he looked back at me with a blank expression.*

"You show progress. Good!" He then attacked me again, but this time I saw his move without needing to squint. I managed to avoid his attack, and the next one, and the next one, and all the other attacks that he executed against me. Then I tried to land a blow to him. That was a huge mistake. As I let my fist soar through the air in a straight line towards the mans face, he grabbed hold of my hand and somehow managed to toss me half way across the compound. As I was flying away from the man I realised that I would have to be more inventive if I was going to defeat him. Then I hit the ground with such force that I made a small crater. I had some difficulties in getting up after the hard impact, but I finally managed to get to my feet again. I turned towards the man just in time it would seem. I saw him moving towards me with such immense speed that a normal eye wouldn't been able to perceive his movements. But for some strange reason I could see his every movement as if he was moving through water. I wasn't complaining over this new sense I had developed, as it was helping me avoid all the attacks from the man. I just had to figure out how to go on the offensive without the risk of being cast through the air again. The man was upon me and I managed to avoid getting his

fist in my face by stepping swiftly to the right. The man followed up the attack with a multitude of incredibly fast hits. I managed to avoid every single one of them. I was getting good at avoiding his attacks now. But how to go on the offensive? The longer I kept avoiding his attacks, the longer and harder did he push them at me. Suddenly as I avoided one of his fists, I managed to spin around him and end up behind him. As I saw him turn towards me, I struck out at him, hitting him on his right cheek. I was surprised to feel my fist make contact with him. But I wasn't going to let up on him, I followed up the lucky punch with a myriad of punches, all hitting their mark. He started to stagger and I was about to deliver a really heavy punch, when he put up his hands and motioned me to stop. It was difficult but I managed to stop myself, don't ask me why I stopped, I could have continued my attack on him and finished him off. But something told me that he was more worth to me alive than dead, so I stopped myself.

He stood panting for a few moments and then composed himself, straightening his clothes and even gave me a brief smile.

"Very well done! You managed to defeat me. I didn't expect you to do it so soon. Now we can start your real training."

The training commenced properly the very next day. The man, who had now given me his name, Sensei Ocul Te, took me for a climb up Mount Fuji. Once we reached the top of the volcano, we ran down. Then we ran for miles and returned late in the evening. This procedure was repeated every day for the next few months. Once I had managed to cut down the time it took to do all this by half, I was made to swim in the lakes that surrounds the volcano. I was getting stronger and Sensei Ocul Te was pleased with my progress. He said that I was to be prepared for dangers that lie ahead.

Months turned to years, years turned to decades and soon enough I had lost all track of time and forgotten about the world outside of where we lived and trained.

One day Sensei Ocul Te summoned me to his building. He was looking very serious.

"My dear student, I believe you are now ready to go out in the world again. It is time for you to take over from me on this world.

My time here is up now." At these last words, I started to object. "Calm down my dear student! What will be, will be and must be. I am to leave this world soon and you are to carry on all my knowledge and take it out in to the world and make sure that you fight for peace, justice and most important, fight for the weak. Now before you go, I have a gift for you." He went over to the table. On the table was a small wooden box. He picked it up and handed it to me. "Open it!" he urged.

I opened the lid and looked inside the box. Inside the box was an object of about two decimetres. I took it out of the box and held it in my hand, making sure to study it very closely. I couldn't for the world figure out what it was. Sensei Ocul Te must have noticed my confusion. "Press that button!" I looked for the button, but couldn't see it at first, but after looking for a few seconds, I located a small button lodged securely in the base of the object. I pushed the button and to my astonishment a long blade extended from it. I looked at it with awe. It was a sword, but like no sword that I had ever seen before. It was narrow and weighed close to nothing. I held it up and then let it swoop through the air, the sword made a high-pitched noise as it cut through the air.

"I made it especially for you. Use it for good, never use it in anger and it will serve you well for your entire life. Now leave me. My time here draws to an end." I started to object, but he was adamant that I should leave him at once. I had no choice. I left him to die there on that chilly October morning.

It was time to head back to Britain.

As I made my way back across China and Europe I noticed how things had changed. Old Kingdoms had fallen and new kingdoms had arisen from the ashes. Nothing was as I could remember it. After several months of walking I found myself on the western coast of Frankish kingdom, looking westwards towards Britain. I managed to get hold of a fisherman who promised me that he could get me across the channel. A few hours later I stood on the shores of Britain once again.

As I trudged up the sand dunes I heard someone scream. I soon saw a man running from some other men. The men that were chasing the screaming man, all wore suits of armour and rode huge horses. The running man passed me by without even daring to offer me a swift glance. I managed to catch a glimpse of his facial expression and saw only pure fear there. The riders galloped past me, almost knocking me over, oblivious to me standing there. I shouted out to them. Half of the men turned their horses around and headed back my way. They reached me soon enough and halted their steeds.

"What have we 'ere?" They did not speak any British that I could understand. It sounded more like a mixture of Frankish and something else, perhaps Saxon or Germanic. I asked them why they were chasing after that man. "'E 'az been stealing from Baron de Rocque, it iz an offenze punishable wiz death."

I asked what the man had stolen. "Eet doez not matter. Any stealing from the Baron is punishable wiz death." I asked them if it was possible for me to meet the Baron and clear this up by paying for whatever the man had stolen. I of course had no gold or anything else to pay the Baron with, but I hoped that he would accept my service as payment. Although I wasn't really sure about working for someone who was so harsh against his subjects. The other riders returned, dragging the scared man behind one of the horses.

"Let uz have little fun with ziz one before 'e dies." I repeated my offer of paying the Baron for whatever the man had stolen. The armour-clad men looked at each other, and I could see in their faces that they were contemplating my offer, but I could see disappointment as well at the prospect of missing out on some fun with the thief.

Finally, one of the men nodded and they let the man go and within a few seconds he had run off. The men motioned to me to follow. I was led down a winding track that led in to a small forest and out to the other side of the forest, where in the not so far distance I could see a castle made of rocks. It was no Camelot, but still pretty impressive.

I was led in through a heavily guarded large gate in to a stone paved court yard.

"Wait 'ere and we will tell ze Baron that you are 'ere." They left me alone in the middle of the court yard which was almost entirely empty, except for some peddlers trying to sell their wares. It didn't take long before the men returned, this time they had a dark haired, tall man with them. He strode up to me and looked me over. "oo are you?" I hadn't really given much thought to names. The last name I had used was Lancelot, but that name felt dated and maybe I should come up with another. I had to give my brain process a hard work out to finally come up with Julius, after the Roman general Julius Caesar.

I gave him my new name and he looked blankly at me. "I 'ear zat you wish to pay for the stolen bread."

Bread? Had it been bread that the man had stolen? And why did that crime result in twelve heavily armed men on horses chasing after him. That seemed absurd. However, I was going to pay for the poor mans crime. I offered my services to the Baron by falling to one knee.

"We 'ave no need for your services. But if you do want to serve, go north to York and seek out the righteous King John. He will need men to fight for him if his brother should return from Jerusalem any time soon.

My story was interrupted by a loud commotion nearby and suddenly Sir Dinadan had approached. Sire, with your permission, I apologise for disturbing you in the middle of Sir Lancelot's story, but there is a large army heading in our direction.

Arthur got up at once. Looks like you will have to finish your story another time Lance. Call to arms! Knights of the table round! To arms! To arms!

It didn't take long for all the knights to get prepared to meet the approaching army. I stood next to Arthur with my sword in my hand, ready to go to battle. Merlin had been and retrieved Excalibur for Arthur and he now stood with it firm in hand, prepared to let the famous sword cut into the enemy.

But as the army drew closer I recognised a man in the crowd. I cried out to the knights to put down their arms. It was Polyphemus and an army of mutants that were coming to join us in the fight against the invaders. The knights were first taken aback by the appearance of the mutants, but once they learned that the mutants had once been humans but become misshapen in the wake of the fire in the skies disaster, their opinions slightly shifted and soon the mutant army was accepted.

Chapter 8

The next morning, we all moved into position on the outskirts of the ruined city of Gothenburg. The plan was to put the knights in the front line and let Polyphemus and the mutants circle around the enemy and fall in behind them as they pushed their attack. Hopefully the enemy had never heard of this manoeuvre, as the whole attack rested on the success on surprising them.

Arthur gave the orders to position the knights in a straight formation, three lines deep. He gave order to blow the horns, and the sound from them reverberated throughout the ruined city. It didn't take long before an army of the invaders was seen leaving the ruins. They positioned themselves across from us and by first glance it seemed as if they outnumbered us seven to one, which gave more reason to hope that our manoeuvre with the mutants was going to work.

Once the enemy had positioned themselves, they started to shout and growl and grunt and make loads of loud guttural sounds, banging their weapons on their shields. The noise was deafening, and the knights answered in kind by blowing their horns and banging their weapons on their shields and shouting taunts at the enemy. Finally, the enemy stopped their noise and started their charge. I braced myself and gave a sideward glance to my right where Arthur stood, wielding Excalibur, which was, in comparison with my own sword, a gigantic piece of sharpened metal. Arthur was concentrating on the oncoming army and I could see that his knuckles were turning white from clutching the handle of Excalibur. I glanced to my left where I could see Jock, wielding his gigantic sledgehammer, and wearing a very worried frown on his visage.

The enemy were getting closer by the second, running in their own specific way, as only beings with short, stubby legs can run. When they had cleared half the distance from their original position to ours, Polyphemus brought in his mutant army in from the enemy's rear. The result was what we had wished for. The enemy army started to panic as the new army crashed into them from behind and we took that as our cue to start our attack. Arthur raised Excalibur into the air and shouted *Knights of the table round, advance!*

And that is exactly what we all did. We advanced on the enemy, who were now so confused by the double attack that they offered little resistance as we crashed into them. A short while afterwards the battle was over, and the entire enemy army lie dead on the ground.

We gathered our troops together and then after doing a head count, we realised that we hadn't lost more than fifteen of the mutant army in the battle. We held a short service for the fallen and then we continued into the ruined city and headed to the portal. We reached the portal without meeting anymore of the enemy. Merlin approached Arthur and told him that we would have to go through the portal to put a stop to it from ever being used again. The plan was to send all the knights through the portal and leave the mutants behind to guard the portal on this side in case any of the enemy were still lingering on Earth.

I stood with Arthur and Merlin at the front of the knights facing the ring-shaped portal. It flickered and showed a slightly distorted view of what we were to expect on the other side. Arthur took a deep breath and then asked Merlin in a whispering voice, that I could hardly hear, *Are you sure about this Merlin?* Merlin smiled and whispered back *It is the only way. Sound the advance Arthur.* Arthur took another deep breath and then raised Excalibur in the air again and shouted as he had done in battle *Knights of the table round, advance!*

Then we took the first steps through the portal. The sensation that followed can only be described as being pulled and stretched like an elastic band, then compressed into a tiny particle, only to be stretched like elastic again. It was a terrible experience and I felt like letting the entire contents of my stomach exit through my mouth. I soon felt ground under my feet again and things had returned to normal, but I still felt as if my stomach wanted to expel its contents. I fell to my knees and realised that I was not alone in

doing this. Everyone that had gone through the portal were down on their knees, releasing their stomach contents on to the ground. All except Merlin, who seemed untouched by the whole sensation. *Get yourselves together, we have a war to win here.* We all got up and started to get our gear in order, still feeling queasy. Over in the distance there was a terrible display of lightning, which seemed to be focused on one area. Arthur gave a very quiet order to advance. I started out, only to find myself being pulled aside by Merlin. *We have another matter to take care of, Black Panther.*
So here it comes, now he is going to get rid of me once and for all. I knew that he didn't like me. Not since I caused the fall of Camelot by bedding Guinevere all those centuries ago. And now at long last, Merlin was going to get rid of me so that Camelot would never again fall from within. I braced myself for his magic blow that was sure to come. But it never did. *We need to head in this direction!* Merlin pointed in a direction almost opposite of the way in which Arthur had taken the knights. I of course asked why we weren't joining Arthur in the upcoming battles. *There's something else we need to do in order to get a victorious outcome of this war.* He then motioned me to follow him as he strode off in giant strides. Still the lightning display in the far distance continued. Merlin strode onwards in silence, despite my attempts of getting answers from him as to where we were going and what we were about to do.
As we were moving towards our mysterious goal, sounds of battle from far behind us reached my ear. I stopped and wanted to turn around and run back to aid Arthur and the knights in the battle, but I was silently and forcefully stopped from doing so by Merlin.
A short while later we were climbing a hill, and once we reached the summit of the hill, I noticed that Merlin had stopped walking, which made me almost crash in to him. I wondered why he had stopped, but he didn't answer me, he only pointed to the distance. I looked in the direction in which he was pointing and saw a huge castle far off in the distance. I asked if that was our goal, Merlin only nodded and then he set off again at a faster pace than earlier. I followed him as fast as I could, but despite my speed not being

lacking in pace, I had difficulties in keeping up with him.

We ran and ran and the castle grew as we got closer to it. It was black, so very black that it seemed to absorb all light around it. It looked as if it was a home for pure evil and nothing else. What awaited us there?

We finally reached the huge black gates of the castle, only to find them locked. Merlin stood in front of them for what seemed like ages and then suddenly with a deafening, grinding sound, the gates were blown off their hinges. Merlin motioned me inside. I entered the black castle and discovered to my dismay that it was equally black inside. There was no light at all, and we ventured onwards in perpetual darkness.

After walking around in the darkness for what seemed like ages, I heard an evil sort of laughter, emanating from somewhere in front of me. That was not Merlin laughing, I was sure of that much any way. But if it wasn't Merlin, who was it? Then, all of a sudden, the room was lit up so bright that I went temporarily blind. I heard voices shouting at each other and realised that one of the voices belonged to Merlin, but I didn't recognise who the owner of the other voice was.

Chapter 9

The shouting voices continued as my eyesight slowly returned, and then finally I could see once again. I saw Merlin and a tall, dark clad man standing, facing each other about two metres in front of me.

Quick Black Panther, attack him! I reacted more out of instinct than anything else and drew my sword and rushed towards the dark clad man. But without any warning, I was hit by some kind of invisible force that knocked me across the room. I landed on the floor with a thud and a groan. What had I been hit by? *Beware his mental pushes! I will try and hold his mental powers at bay, as long as you attack him physically.* I wasn't going to question Merlin on this issue, the dark clad man had some powerful mental pushes and needed to be dealt with at once. I felt a nudge of the same type of invisible force that had hit me earlier, but this time, I guessed that Merlin was fighting him on a mental level, keeping me safe from more of those mental attacks.

I jumped in between Merlin and the dark clad man with my sword raised. I charged the dark clad man but before I could make contact with him, he moved out of the way and drew a sword of his own, which was so huge that it dwarfed Excalibur, not to mention my toothpick-sized sword.

He attacked and I just managed to get my sword up to defend myself from the blow. When the blades clashed, they sung out and sparks flew in all directions. What followed after that initial attack was more or less a blur for me. The dark clad man moved like a whirlwind and pushed his attacks at me with ferocity, meanwhile I could feel the nudges of his mental pushes that Merlin was deflecting.

I felt that I was out of my league in this fight, the dark clad man was not only a fiendishly good fighter with a sword, he was also a great master of the same kind of magic powers that Merlin knew. I knew that if it hadn't had been for Merlin, I wouldn't have stood a chance in this fight. I glanced at Merlin and I could see him sweating heavily. It looked as if he was using every single erg of his powers to keep me safe. That is when I stumbled over a chair

and fell to the floor. I dropped my sword and it slid across the floor to the other side of the room. Within microseconds the dark clad man was standing over me, ready to strike me down with his gigantic sword. I panicked. I wanted to push him away, far away from me, in order to give me a chance to get to my feet and retrieve my sword. But what happened next, surprised not only me and the dark clad man, but also, it would seem, Merlin. The dark clad man was flung away from me and hit the wall on the opposite side of the room with a loud thud. He fell to the floor, but was soon on his feet again, rushing towards me. I quickly got to my feet and hurled myself in the direction of my sword, managed to get a grip on the handle while doing a somersault which landed me on my feet with my back against the charging dark clad man. I spun around and then it happened again. My wish was to push him, and it happened, he flew across the room and struck the wall once again. This time he wasn't as quick in getting up as he had been the first time. *Keep doing what you are doing Black Panther! Keep pushing him! Don't let up, whatever you do, don't let up!* I had somehow thought that it had been Merlin doing the pushing, but his words seemed to imply that it was I that was doing the mental pushing. I just wasn't sure as to how exactly I was doing it. Then as the dark clad man was getting close to me again, it happened once more. I pushed him. I pushed him hard. It sounded as if something broke in his body this time when he slammed into the wall. He got up slowly and I could see blood trickling from his mouth. He was staggering now, having problems with his breathing. He turned towards Merlin, I prepared to attack. *You have taught him well, son of Lucifer. But this changes nothing. My revenge will be complete, even in my death, because you will not find what you search for.* Then he laughed, and more blood squirted out of his mouth. I pushed at him again and this time he had difficulties in getting up again. When he finally got up again, he was moving like a punch-drunk boxer.
Finish him off! The only way to kill someone like us is to cut out the heart. Do it now!
Someone like us? What did he mean? No! No time to think about

that now, this man needs to be stopped. He sent the army through the portal to invade Earth. If he can't be stopped, then he might enslave all of Earths population, as it is. I rushed over to him and let my sword penetrate his chest plate. Once the sword had gone into his chest and out the other side, I thrust my hand in to the hole in his chest and soon found his warm, beating heart. I glanced at Merlin. *Pull it out!* I turned my attention to the dark clad man. Blood was gushing from his wounds and he looked as if he was already dead. But then he turned his gaze upon me and there was recognition in his eyes. *I... I know you.* He said those words at the same instant that I pulled his beating heart from his chest. Did he know me? Now it was too late to ask him if he really knew me or if he had just been so close to death that he thought that I was someone else that he had known in his past. But now I would never know. His dead body slumped to the floor and I stood over him, still holding his warm heart in my hand. I dropped it and it hit the floor with a smacking sound. I fell to my knees next to his lifeless body, not knowing why killing this man had made me feel this way. Maybe it was because he had said, in his dying breath, that he knew me. Perhaps it was because the fight had taken so much out of me. Maybe it was because he had been an immortal being like me and now I had killed him. Whatever the reason was for my feelings it caused tears to fall down my face. Merlin walked up to me, bent down and picked up the heart. He then commenced to conjure up a fire and threw the heart on it. *Separating the heart from the body is not always enough to kill one of us. Always better to burn the heart. If the heart lives on, then there is always chance for the owner to be reunited with it. But without the heart there is no hope. Without hope, death is more welcome. Remember that well Black Panther, do not lose heart.*

Merlin then turned his attention away from me and seemed to go into a trance. He stood still for more than ten minutes and then finally moved again. *There!* He said and pointed a long finger at a partition of a wall, then he headed off in that direction. I followed him even though he moved so much faster than I could ever do. We moved silently down winding stairs and I couldn't help but wonder how huge the castle was. The darkness that had been ever present as we had made our way into the castle was diminishing bit by bit and I could see my surroundings and marvel at the murals that decorated the walls and ceilings. Ever we moved downwards, down the ever-winding stairs. Then suddenly Merlin stopped, and I almost ran right into him, but managed to stop myself in the last second. He sniffed the air and looked around, and then walked slowly down the last few steps to the stone floor that awaited us. He looked around and motioned towards a wooden door, it was one of many wooden doors in the vicinity. Merlin walked over to the door and said a few words that made the huge metal lock burst open and the door swung open. It took a few seconds before a figure emerged from the dark room that had been on the inside of the locked door. The figure was a man. A tall man with dark, long hair bunched together in a ponytail. He wore a goatee which suited him, as his face was gaunt. He stumbled out of the dark room, squinting his eyes as he wasn't used to the bright light.

Father!

I was taken aback, what had Merlin just said?

Father, I've come to rescue you.

I was confused, was this tall man Merlin's father? Somehow, I had never imagined Merlin having natural parents, I had imagined him being, not born, but sort of, created or something else magical, but not actually having a father and a mother. It just shattered my entire picture of him.

The tall man tried to focus on the direction of Merlin's voice and stumbled over to where Merlin was standing.

Merlin? Is that really you?

The man staggered and was about to fall and hit the floor, but Merlin managed to catch him as he fell.

It is I, father. I have come to bring you back home.

Merlin held the man in an embrace, the man hugged him back and kept blinking as if to try and get used to bright light. Finally, he stopped blinking and looked straight at Merlin. A smile crossed his lips as he saw Merlin.

Merlin, I am so glad to see you. It has been so long since I last cast my gaze upon your visage.

Merlin seemed a bit reserved but still held on firmly to his father. They stood linked together for some time and then dislodged themselves. Merlin's father now turned his gaze upon me, and I felt a bit unsettled as his eyes met mine. Who was this man? He walked over to me and I guessed that I would soon find out.

He circled me, looking me over from head to toe and this unsettled me even more. Finally, he stopped circling and came to a halt in front of me. He looked me straight into my eyes and stared into them for what seemed like an eternity. I tried to avert my eyes but found that I couldn't move, my whole body felt as if it was filled with concrete. Then he released our eye contact and my body was once again my own. The man smiled.

I'm sorry, I thought you were someone else. But I was mistaken. Hmm, perhaps I was mistaken, perhaps not. That is something to ponder on. Oh, I'm sorry I am so rude. Please allow me to introduce myself, I am man of wealth and taste. I have had many names cast upon me, but let us use the one that was mine from the beginning and the one that I favour most of all. Please call me Lucifer. And you are?

Lucifer? What? THE Lucifer? No that couldn't be possible, it just couldn't be possible. Could it? I hesitated, long enough for Lucifer to react to my hesitation.

He laughed, long and loud, and the laughter was just a bit terrifying. Then he stopped laughing and looked at me once again. *I know what you think, everyone thinks it when they meet me. Do I want your soul? The answer is, of course I don't want your soul, what would I do with it. That is some strange notion that humans have made up over the years. Made me out as a bad guy, while all I really am is a very misunderstood man with a bad PR department, unlike my friend who is…*

Lucifer trailed off as he mentioned his friend. He snapped his fingers and walked over to another wooden door with a huge metal lock.

Merlin, would you please get this lock open.

Merlin shook his head and refused to even go near the door.

Oh, come on Merlin, my powers are still weak from my time in prison, I could of course use force on the lock and open it that way, but it would take longer time than your magic. Come on Merlin, please! I beg of you, can't you do it for me at least?

Merlin hesitated and then reluctantly walked over to the door, looked at his father and then uttered a few words making the lock break and the wooden door swung wide open.

A figure emerged from the dark room, he was somewhat shorter than Lucifer, had long, blond hair, but no facial hair. He blinked at the bright light.

Lucifer walked over to him and embraced him. The blond man looked surprised, he couldn't really see anything yet, but I think he understood who it was embracing him.

Luce, is that you?

Lucifer nodded and then realised how stupid that had been as his friend still couldn't see properly.

Aye, it's me, we have been rescued by my son and this… stranger over there. He pointed over in my direction and was struck again by the stupidity of his gestures to a man that didn't have use of his eyes.

Soon the blond man stopped blinking and took a long look at Lucifer. He smiled, then he turned his gaze at Merlin and his smile disappeared, he looked at Merlin for a long time and then he shifted his gaze upon me. His look changed from the annoyed look that he had been wearing whilst looking at Merlin to a look of surprise and bewilderment.

Who have we here?

He walked over to me and did the same routine that Lucifer had done earlier, but this time when he stopped and looked me in the eyes I didn't experience the same feeling of being filled with concrete as I had done when Lucifer had looked me in the eyes. Whoever this man was, he was of a gentler nature than Lucifer. He then released his grip on me and smiled at me.

Who are you? I thought I recognised you at first, but after closer scrutiny I realised that you were not who I thought you to be. So, who are you?

I was surprised, Lucifer had thought that he knew me at first, but then realised that he had been wrong, now this blond man thought that he knew me. What was going on?

Father, this man here is James Best also known as The Black Panther, also known under many different names during the years he's inhabited Earth. He was known as Lancelot during my time with Arthur, if you remember.

Lucifer nodded and so did the blond man.

Ah yes, I remember Lancelot, one of the knights of the table round who went out on the quest for the Holy Grail all those years ago. Let me introduce myself, My name is Yahweh, although I don't go by as many names as my friend Luce does, I am known as Allah to some people.

Allah? Now I was more confused than ever. I could swallow the fact that I had the devil standing in front of me, but having God himself stand there as well, no, that was too much for me to understand or even be able to accept.

You look confused young man, please don't be. I know it must be difficult for you to meet your creator. Although I can't really remember creating you. Anyway, I think that we should get out of Lord Sachka's castle and return home.

That was the best thing I had heard in a long time. Though my mind was filled with loads of unanswered questions, they could just as easily be answered back on Earth.

We made our way out of the castle and headed back to the portal that would take us to Earth. On the way we met up with Arthur and the Knights. They too had been victorious in their battle, all the enemy were either dead or sent scattered across the land.

Once we reached the portal, Merlin activated it and we all filed through. I was just about to go through when Merlin grabbed me by my arm. I tried to shake him loose, but his grip on me was too firm. He spun me around, so I was facing him. He looked troubled. *I must remain here Black Panther.* At first, I didn't understand what he had just said. Then it dawned on me, but I couldn't understand why. *The portal must be destroyed! And that can only be done from this side. You need to go back to Earth. I will remain here and make sure this portal is never used again.* I began to say: *in that case it should be me that remained behind,* but Merlin wasn't having it, he muttered a few words and all of a sudden I felt myself hurtling towards the portal. Soon enough I was sucked in it and the nauseating sensation that I had felt previously made an unwanted comeback.

Chapter 10

I turned towards the portal and prepared myself to go back to get Merlin, but before I could take a step, the shimmer in the portal died and the path to the other world was severed forever. As I was already heading towards the portal when it got shut down, I was treated to a small flight through the large ring, falling flat on my face on the other side of it. I felt the taste of sand and dirt in my mouth as I managed to get to my feet. I looked at the knights and I could see confusion in their expressions. I guess they were wondering about my actions. Arthur strode over to me, with a furious look on his face. *Where is Merlin?* He demanded. I initially tried to avoid his staring eyes, but finally I raised my head and looked him directly in his eyes and told him what had happened. It seemed to take a few moments for what I had said to sink in. Then suddenly it was if his fury was gone, in its stead came sadness. Arthur sank down into a sitting position on the ground. *Gone?* He said, repeatedly. I walked away, slightly dazed. What a day this had turned out to be. The other knights remained silent, probably contemplating their fate now that Merlin no longer was there to help them.

I was sitting on the edge of the ruined city, looking out westwards on the barren wasteland that once had been an ocean. I was lost in thought, so I wasn't aware that Yahweh and Lucifer were approaching me. I gave a slight startled jump when I felt a hand on my shoulder. I got up and twisted around in a simultaneous manoeuvre and came face to face with the two guys we had rescued. The two guys that claimed to be God and the Devil. Hard to believe that kind of thing really.
I understand this must be difficult for you. I can see in your face what you are thinking. You don't believe that I am God and that Lucifer, here, is the Devil. I think I can remedy that. Behold!
He muttered a few words. Suddenly something started to happen. I wasn't sure what was happening at first, but it soon became clear. Earth was returning to its former glory. Grass was growing, trees popped up out from the ground, water returned, and the air was suddenly bustling with life. I swatted my first fly in years, before

realising what I had done. I looked at Yahweh and Lucifer in bewilderment. *Behold Earth as it was and how it should be. The cities of Earth have not been rebuilt. That is something that the humans must do by themselves, if they so wish. Now I must be off home, I have been gone too long.* He then muttered a word and took a step to the left and vanished into thin air. *I too must go home.* Lucifer muttered a few words, took a step to the left and he too vanished, leaving me alone once again.

I looked out across, what only minutes ago had been a wasteland, and was astonished by the beauty of the green forests and the blue of the ocean. The sound of birds singing reached my ears and it was so foreign to me that I didn't realise what it was at first. Once I had come to terms with that Earth was back to good form again, I started dancing around, singing at the top of my voice, proclaiming how wonderful and beautiful everything was.

I was suddenly aware that I wasn't alone. I turned around and saw Arthur and all he knights standing, watching me. I stopped dancing and singing and tried to compose myself. Arthur strode over to me and I could see that his sadness was still present but there was also a look of bemusement. *What happened here Lance? How did this happen?* I let my eyes wander towards the sky, but remained silent, instead I just shrugged my shoulders. Didn't think it would be any point telling what had really happened. Would they even believe me? Then I smiled and said that we should be happy that everything is back to the way it should be. Now it is up to us to start to rebuild any structures that we might need or want. Arthur looked at me, then he smiled. *Camelot! We can rebuild Camelot! And this time Camelot will not fall!* He shook his fist at the skies. *You hear me? This time it will not fall!* He turned back to his knights and raised both his hands into the air. *Knights, this is a glorious day indeed. We can restore the glory of Camelot.* Then he paused and it seemed as if he was growing sad again, his shoulders seemed to sag. He remained like that for a few moments, and then he straightened up again and raised his hands in to the air again. *It is both a glorious and sad day today. Sad because we have lost Merlin, but a glorious day, because the war is over. We won! We can now get on with the restoration of Camelot! Are you with me?* All the knights raised their hands into the air and released an ear-deafening roar. The roar lasted for what felt like ages and then it died down, but only for a few seconds, then the knights roared again. Five more roars were released from them until Arthur silenced them by putting up his hands in a stopping gesture. He turned towards me again. *And you? What about you, Lance? Are you with me? Hm?* I really didn't want to be a part of the whole Camelot experience once more. Especially after what happened last time. Arthur seemed so sure that Camelot wouldn't fall this time, but I didn't believe that. Another Guinevere might come between us. Would he forgive me this time? Would he forgive me if I didn't join him? The decision was difficult, but I finally reached one. Not an easy one, but there weren't going to be any easy decisions this time. I told him that I would be there if times were dire and there were no other solutions. He looked disappointed, and I could relate to that. I would have been disappointed too if the shoe had been on the other foot.

I'll hold you to it, you know! I nodded. I knew that he would. Any large attack on Camelot and he would call for me, wherever I might be at the time. He then turned from me again and returned to his knights. They released yet another roar. I turned away from them and decided that I should go and visit my old friend William. He did have a Tavern, and that would mean a nice soft bed to sleep on and food on the table. But how would I get there now? There was an ocean between Sweden and England that hadn't been here the last few times that I travelled between the two countries. I would have to try and make a boat or something else that would float on water.

Making a boat proved to be more difficult than I had initially thought. I ended up making a raft instead and said a silent prayer that it would carry me safely across the ocean to my destination. It was a beautiful sunny day when I launched my raft, cleverly christened Kon Tiki, and set off on my long and most likely dangerous voyage.

I had made sure that I had put handles on the raft for me to be able to hold on, if it should get rough out there. And it didn't take long before I needed to use them. I was two days away from the coast of Sweden when a very bad storm hit the area that I was in. As soon as the electrical storm started, so did the high waves. I held on to the handles for dear life as the raft was being tossed from side to side in the storm and I had no chance of steering it in my intended direction. I would usually be feeling sick from the motion at sea, but since my recent experience with travelling through the portal I must have been rendered slightly immune to something so mundane as sea sickness.

I am not sure how long the storm lasted for, but once it was over, I had no idea where I was. I had no idea how to navigate by stars or sun, other than the sun rose in the east and set in the west. But if the storm had taken me too far out of course, I could be drifting around, lost, forever.

At least a week went by without any sign of land, but on the positive side, there were no more storms, but on the negative side, the sun was baking me. I thought I was hallucinating when I heard voices coming towards me. I looked in the direction the voices seemed to come from and was surprised to see a ship heading in my direction, or was it just a hallucination? I couldn't be sure, but, yes, it was indeed a ship and it was really heading in my direction. I stood up and started waving my arms, hoping that they would notice me. The ship soon caught up with my raft and I looked up at the faces of the people on board, to my surprise I looked into the faces of Sir Gawain and Sir Tristan. They extended their hands to help me onboard their ship. *Going our way Lance?* They both laughed heartily, and Tristan gave me a cup of hot chocolate. I downed the chocolate in several gulps and handed the cup back to Tristan. I thanked him for both the chocolate and the rescue. *What were you thinking? Travelling on the high seas on a small raft, a bit reckless, even for you.* I just smiled at him.

They were heading for England, to build Camelot and recreate the golden age that once had been, so very long ago. Arthur came and sat down next to me on the small bench where I was sitting, drinking the hot chocolate. *You know, that when you turned me down, I was furious. I wanted everything to be like before. Then I realised that you were not ready to return to my court. Not after what happened at the end of all that was.* He was not entirely wrong, not entirely right either. *We fell in love with the same woman and she came in-between us, and that should never have happened.* I told him that things might not be exactly the way it had been before, but I would be there for him if he needed me. He smiled and assured me that was enough for him, but if I should change my mind, then I would be welcome back to court.

The rest of the voyage took us across a calm Norse sea and we finally saw the coast of England in the far distance. Once we reached the shores we said our farewells and I set off to find William and his Tavern. I wasn't sure where it was, but at least I had an idea that it was close to where Sherwood Forest had been once upon a time. That would be the direction I would head in first.

Sherwood Forest, now that was a place that had stuck in my memory.

I had left Baron de Rocque a few weeks back and was heading for York to meet King John and offer him my services. I reached the small town of Nottingham and stopped overnight in a Tavern at the foot of the Castle. The next day, as the sun rose, I set off north towards York. The road eventually led me to a forest that looked dark and dense. I commenced to walk through it. I hadn't been in the forest more than perhaps ten minutes when I saw someone on the ground. I increased my pace to reach the person. I bent down and saw that the person was lying face down, I turned the person around and saw that it was a young man. I wondered what had happened here. But before I had a chance to come up with any kind of solution to the mystery, the young man opened his eyes and smiled as he brought up his hand, brandishing a dagger, into my gut. I let out a low grunt as the knife hit home but managed to get to my feet, prepared to take on the young man. He also stood up now and looked at me in triumph. "Hand over your money lest you want me to give you another stab." He smiled again. I made a move towards him, thinking that this wouldn't take long. But the young man stood still, and still smiling he lifted his right arm and pointed in my direction, or rather he pointed to something behind me. I stopped my charge and looked back and saw a large group of men standing there, all of them were armed with bows and had arrows pointing towards me. The young man spoke again. "You might want to consider your next move, carefully." I knew that I would be able to take them all on, but something about them reminded me of the man that I had saved a few weeks back, the bread thief who had been hunted by twelve heavily armoured knights. I raised my hands into the air and told them that I wouldn't be causing them any trouble. Out of the group a man came forward, he walked up to me and stood close. He stood and stared at me for a very long time and then finally broke out in a smile and laughed. "I believe you might be a troublesome man, but for whom? Now, that is the question, isn't it? Do you believe in justice? If you do, then I suggest you think twice about what justice is." I must have looked as confused as I felt, because he laughed again. "Do you believe in the justice of the law or the justice of the people?" I still wasn't sure what he was getting at. Suddenly a man rushed up and interrupted us. I realised that I recognised him. He was the bread thief from a few weeks ago. "Robin! I know this man! Please don't hurt him! He was the one that I was telling you about, you know, the man that saved me from Baron de Rocque's knights a few weeks back while I was still living in the south. He saved my life! Don't hurt him, please!" The man that had been named Robin looked at the bread thief for a short while then turned his gaze upon me once again. "I see you believe in justice after all." He smiled and laughed again. "You are welcome to join us if you wish, we don't have much to offer, except a life on the run, and a nice forest to live in. What say you?" I thought that if the King had Barons serving him that would hunt down men that stole bread, then what kind of King would he be? These men *seemed to be victims of a corrupt society. The decision wasn't difficult. I joined.*

It turned out that they did indeed live in the forest and their camp was well hidden within the dense woods, if you didn't know it was there you would just as easily walk right past it. Their leader was the man that had looked me over, he was called Robin Hood, but I soon learned that he had been a noble before, an Earl or something like that, but the Norman invaders had driven him away from his land and he had joined forces with other victims of the invaders, to form this gang of outlaws that lived on stealing from rich travellers.

The biggest threat to the freedom of this motley crew was a man called William de Wendenal, who acted as a peacekeeper of sorts in this region of the land. His greatest desire was to put a stop to Robin Hood and the menace of the outlaws of Sherwood Forest. Of course, a showdown between the two men would be inevitable, but who would be the victor in such a combat? Now that was a good question. I know that legends and especially movie makers had Robin Hood and the entire gang lay siege to the castle in Nottingham, but that never happened. It would have been plain suicide to even attempt an attack on that castle, the hill leading up to it was more than sufficient to slow any attackers from ever reaching the walls. The showdown eventually took place on the plains outside of the forest. It was a magnificent battle. Robin had placed his best archers in the forest and then he himself led the assault on de Wendenal's forces. The entire battle was confusing and by the end of it most of de Wendenal's soldiers were lying dead on the ground. Robin was missing and the remainder of his men fled as we saw Prince John riding towards us in front of a large force of cavalry. I had to get away from there as well, so I fled back into the forest. Robin was nowhere to be found and only a handful of his men had made it back to camp. No one knew what had happened to Robin, we had to succumb to the thought that he had been killed in the battle. The next decision we had to make was if we were going to continue fighting for our freedom or disband and let it be each man for himself. I could see that the fight had

been knocked out of them all and they soon came to an agreement
that we should disband. And thus, ended the real tale of Robin
Hood and his Merry men. A story later changed by troubadours
and storytellers to make it all more exciting and romantic than it
really was. They even invented the character of Maid Marion, she
however, at least to my knowledge, never existed.

As my mind stopped reminiscing, I found that my feet had brought
me to my destination, in front of me stood the Tavern, The Green
Hornet once again. I entered.

Chapter 11

I went up to the wooden bar that stood at the far end of the big room. Once I reached it, I called out for William. It took a few minutes until he emerged from a doorway that led to the kitchen. When he saw me, he broke out in a broad smile. *James! How good to see you again, alive and well. How did the war on the alien invaders fare?* He motioned for me to sit down on one of the wooden benches, incidentally the same one that I had sat on the first time that I was here. I sat down and so did William.
Now James, I want to hear everything that has happened since you left here to go to Stonehenge.

It took an hour or so for me to tell everything that had passed since I had last been here. William listened closely to my story and seemed especially interested in the part about the portal to another world. He confirmed this once I had finished my story.
James, do you realise how lucky you are? I probably looked more confused than anything. Lucky? Me? In what way? *You've been to another world. And you used a portal to travel there. A kind of controlled worm hole.* I must have looked even more confused. And probably even more so when William started on about bending space and time with the help of these portals. I wasn't sure what he was talking about, I was just glad that I was sitting here drinking a nice pint of ale.

Time went by and the late afternoon soon became early evening. We were still sitting at the table, talking about things of the past. One thing that I observed though, was that William would not say anything about what happened to him between the Second World War and ending up here as a tavern keeper. Not a word. I wondered if I should ask him. I decided to let it keep for the time being. Maybe once I had had a few more pints of ale I would just blurt it out and then there would be no taking it back.

William kept pouring us new pints of ale and I started to feel as if I needed to go to the toilet. I got up and headed to the private room.

What a relief, but why was the floor moving in such a strange fashion? Despite the room moving around me I managed to get back to the wooden bench again. And then I blurted.

For a moment William looked shocked. Then it looked as if he became embarrassed. He lowered his eyes and stared at the table in front of him for simply ages. Then he looked to the left and then to the right. Anything to avoid looking straight at me. What was it that made him act in this way? What could possibly be so terrible that he couldn't tell me what had happened. Then it seemed as if he was gathering up all his courage to tell me. He looked up at me and for a few fleeting moments his eyes were trying to avoid any contact with mine. Then he forced himself to calm down.

Ok James, I guess I owe it to you to tell you what happened to me, after all you have told me everything that you experienced.

He paused, and then swallowed loudly. *When the explosives were set in the fortress, I tried to make it out. Like you, I never made it. The explosives detonated and the blast threw me several yards and slammed me into a concrete wall. I think I heard my collarbone snap on impact. Then, as I was lying on the floor, I heard the Royal Navy open fire and then the concrete ceiling came tumbling down upon me. I was knocked unconscious, although I must have thought that I was dead. Anyway...* He paused. *The next thing I know is that I'm waking up, but I'm not buried in concrete, I'm in a bed and it looks as if I am in a hospital. A nurse is standing crouching over another bed, probably tending a patient in it. I try and utter a word, but all that leaves my mouth is a kind of guttural groan. The nurse turns around and looks at me, she smiles, oh how I remember that smile, it still keeps me going you know. That smile. She came over to my bed and said some incomprehensible words, I think she was speaking English, but for some reason I couldn't understand a word of what she was saying. After a short while she left me and came back with a doctor. He spoke the same type of incomprehensible words as the nurse and I started to doubt if it truly was English they were speaking. Maybe it was German? I could understand that they were asking me questions, but they must have thought me an idiot or something as I showed no signs of understanding them. The doctor said something to the nurse and she left the room, only to come back in with a syringe. I wanted to object, but it was to no avail. The nurse injected me with something that knocked me out within the course of a minute. When I awoke again the nurse was standing next to my bed. She asked me, in plain English, if I felt any better. I told her that I understand her now, how come I couldn't understand her before? She said that the explosion, which by the way I had been very lucky to survive, had probably given me a severe concussion and that had caused the speech recognition centre in my brain to become jumbled. She explained that I was in a British Royal Navy field hospital and had been for more than a month. A month? - Was my immediate thought and reply. She smiled at me and said that I should be happy that I survived the explosion and the bombardment that followed.*

I spent the next few days, eating and getting stronger. The nurse and the doctor would come in and visit me and talk with me. One day I had a visitor. He wore the uniform of a General and had medals all over his chest. What a show-off, if you ask me. He sat himself down next to me and asked me how I was. We talked about this, that and the other for a very long time. Then he asked me if I felt well enough to get back in the fight against Germany again. I said that I would be ready in about a day or two. He thought that sounded good, but then proceeded to tell me that I wasn't going to return to piloting. I objected as loudly as I felt was prudent. He just looked blankly at me while I uttered my objections. He then told me that he was heading up a new department within the government where we would be developing new weapons to use against the Germans. He had heard that I was a bit of a technical prodigy and that was exactly the kind of man he needed to bring into this project. I must say that I really didn't know what to respond. He told me that he would be back the next day, in order for me to think about it, as he put it.

Well I can tell you James, the decision was difficult. I loved flying planes, and the thought of not being able to do that, well that was unthinkable. On the other hand, I was educated in physics, chemistry, mathematics and biology. That would be something for me to fall back on once the war was over, but here was a man with an offer for the here and now. A decision had to be made. I was awake all night, tossing, and turning, trying to decide. By the time the first rays of the sun came in through the cracks of the blinds, I had made my mind up. It wasn't long before the General entered the room and walked over to my bed. This time he didn't waste any time on small talk. He got straight to the point. I already knew my answer, but it took some time for me to get it out. My mouth was dry, and the words were sticking in my mouth. Finally, I gave up trying to speak and nodded my answer to the General. He smiled and handed me a single piece of paper, I took it from him and read it. It was consent to secrecy. He motioned me to sign it at the bottom and handed me a pen so that I could sign. I suddenly realised that I might be in too deep. All that secrecy, and cloak and dagger was a bit too much for me. It wasn't me, if you know what I mean. But now it was too late. I had signed away my life. In retrospect, you could probably say that I made a deal with the devil.

After I had signed the consent form, he told me that a transport would be supplied to collect me the next day, and bring me to my new place of work. He then saluted me, smiled, turned away from me and left the room.

I was left with my thoughts and regrets. I tried to persuade myself that I had made the right decision and that it would all be for the best. I had problems believing myself.

William paused for a long time and I could see that tears were lingering in the corner of his eyes. After several minutes of silence, he composed himself and cleared his throat.

Sorry about that, the memories are (pause, he cleared his throat again) *painful, to say the least.*

The next day a man came in to see me, he said that he was the driver that was going to get me to the airfield. I got dressed and followed him out to a car, that was waiting outside the field hospital. I got in and then we headed off towards the closest airfield.

There was a small plane that was going to take me to England, small but it had enough fuel for the entire journey. It was small, I was told, in order to avoid detection. If that was the reason or not, we reached England in one piece. We landed at Biggin Hill airfield, and I got into another car that was waiting there for me. And this is where things started to really freak me out. The car started to speed up, it went faster than anything that I had ever travelled in before, and I've flown Hurricanes. This was faster than the fighter plane, if possible. Yet it was possible, we were zooming across the English countryside at speeds unheard of and I had no idea where we were. Suddenly the driver was heading for a huge wall of rock that made-up part of a cliff. I wanted to shout out to the driver to stop. Stop for the love of God! But I was too scared. I put my hands in front of my eyes but at that moment we passed in through the cliff, unscathed. I was speechless. What had happened? Were we dead? Was this what it felt like to be dead? But we weren't dead, were we. We were very much alive and heading down a long and dark tunnel.

We travelled down the dark tunnel for what felt like hours until we finally reached a circular shaped room. The car came to a sudden halt in the middle of the room. I let out a breath of relief. I was just about to open the door and step out of the car when the driver motioned me not to leave the vehicle. We sat in silence for a few minutes and then suddenly there were clanking noises outside and then the circular room disappeared, and we were hurtling downwards into more darkness, on some sort of platform. I left my stomach and my heart up in the circular room. But once we came to a sudden halt at our destination my heart and stomach caught up with me again. But I was feeling sick and just wanted to get out of the car and throw up. Yet again we sat still in silence in the car and I could but wonder if we were going to travel again in some odd direction. But after a few minutes a mechanical voice outside the car informed us that air pressure levels where now at the same *level as on the surface, and that it was safe to exit the car. The driver got out and came over to my door and opened it. I got out on very shaky legs and threw up, all over the clean floor.*

I was led through a door into a small room. At the other end of the room was another door that I got led through. That door led to a long and sterile looking passage with mediocre lighting. Every step that we took on the floor echoed for what seemed like an eternity. We finally reached yet another door at the end of the passage and I was ushered through it without a word. The driver remained behind in the passage and I found myself alone in a room that was furnished with two chairs and a table and nothing else, no decorations on the walls or curtains, mainly because there were no windows in the room that could benefit from curtains. Suddenly I realised that I wasn't alone in the room anymore. The General was sitting on one of the chairs motioning me to sit myself down on the other one. I hadn't noticed him enter the room, nor had I noticed any other entrance than the one from which I had come in. I turned to look at that door to reassure myself that no one could have got by me from that direction, but to my surprise, the door was no longer there. Now I was more confused than ever, what was going on? The General motioned me once again to sit down on the other chair, this time his smile was missing. I did as he wished. We sat in silence for several minutes and I started to feel very uncomfortable. The General smiled at me again and cocked his head to the right. This made me feel even more uncomfortable and I think that he was enjoying seeing me squirm. Finally, he spoke. "I guess you are wondering what this is all about." I nodded slowly. "Good! An inquisitive mind is a working mind. I thought that I may have made a mistake of taking you on, but I think that you will be most beneficial to our cause. Very beneficial indeed. We need you to work on weapons that we can use on the enemies and I think that your expertise in, not only the fields of natural science, but also your skills at piloting will come in handy." He smiled again and I think that I started to feel more at ease at that point.

I was shown to a lab and explained that this would be my

workplace, and when I asked what it would be that I would be doing, the General answered me that for a start I would be designing rockets that would be sent against the enemy. I remember thinking at the time that this is what war has come to now, we don't even have to see the enemies anymore or even be in the same country. All we have to do is push a button and a rocket will launch and blow up whatever target that has been designated it. But I didn't complain, this was going to give me ample opportunity to put my skills to use, and also be able to take the fight to the Germans. That thought alone pleased me.

Weeks turned in to months, at least I think they did. I had no idea at all how long I had been working in the lab. There were no windows that far underground. I had no clock and no calendar, all I could rely on was the clock in my brain. Also, the fact that I had finished my work on the rockets and was now assigned another project. The new project was to produce the ultimate soldier and then mass produce him. I started to work on robotics, hoping that this would be the solution that I was hoping for. I had read enough science fiction comics as a young boy to know that robots could be a force to be reckoned with. But to build a robot that was as agile, or even more so, as a human being was difficult to say the least. After a few failed attempts, I created Andrew. Andrew was a giant of a robot, twice the size of a normal man, at least to begin with. I managed to get him to walk like a normal human being and not stiff legged as he had done to begin with.

The General would come in several times a week, or something like that, I knew it couldn't be everyday. He would ask me how I was progressing with the robots. I told him that it was going slowly as it was a difficult task to get something dead to act like a human. He told me that I would have to get a move on or else the war might be over, and the enemies might have won before we could get our robot in to the fighting. I promised to get Andrew ready soon enough. I worked non-stop until I had managed to shrink the size of Andrew so that he more or less resembled a normal human being. His components were also shrunk but they still worked, and I would almost say that they worked better in smaller form than they had done when they were big. I also installed cameras in Andrews's eyes, so that I could transmit images from the outside world to my computer screen. It had been a long time since I had seen the outside world, I wasn't sure how long, but it must have been a year or so at the least, and I was curious as to how the war was going. The General was very tight-lipped when it came to matters about the war and the outside world.

Then came the day when I was finally finished with Andrew, I took a step back and looked at him. What a masterpiece, he looked perfect, I don't think that there would be anyone who would think that he wasn't human. I called for the General to come and look at what I had produced. It took him less than a minute to enter my lab after I called him on the intercom. He walked over to Andrew and looked him over. "Does he work?" I nodded. The General continued studying Andrew and touched him in different places to assure himself that it was indeed metal underneath the skin. "Excellent William, excellent! Now get him some clothes and let us send him outside." I supplied Andrew with some clothes and then he was taken from me.

Weeks became months, or at least I'm sure they did. I was totally oblivious to what was going on, and it wasn't even of my own choice. Well, it kind of was, I had agreed to help in the war and this was the price that I had to pay in order to contribute to us winning against the Germans.

I often spent my time staring at a screen, a computer screen it was called, at least that is what the General had told me. It had been a great help in my creation of Andrew. I often wondered what Andrew was up to, I guessed that he would be in Europe somewhere fighting German soldiers. I just wished that I could somehow see him again, or at least see what he could see. Then a thought struck me, I had designed his optics to be able to be viewed remotely. All I had to do was to access that program from my computer and I should be able to access Andrews's optics. After many failed attempts, I finally managed to access the remote optics program and it took me a few minutes to manage to access the optics. A moving image came up on my screen and I soon *realised it was what Andrew was looking at. But he wasn't fighting Germans somewhere in Europe, instead he seemed to be in a city somewhere, where exactly I couldn't tell as I couldn't see any known landmarks, and people that where walking around were dressed in strange colourful clothes and more than one person had flowers in their hair. If that was anything to go by it would seem that the war was over, but I needed to be sure. I needed to know and I tried to use the optics program to override Andrew and steer him to something that would be able to tell me what was going on. I managed to take control of him and steered him into a newsagent. I made him look at The Times and saw that the date on it stated it to be 1967. I almost fell out of my chair. 1967? That would mean that I had been here for more than twenty years and I was fifty years old. I looked at my hands and they did not look like the hands of a fifty-year-old man. I needed to find a mirror and look at my reflection, but I had never seen any mirror since I arrived here all those years ago. I went over to my workbench and started rummaging through all the junk that I had on it and after looking for an extended time I finally found what I was looking for. It was a shiny piece of aluminium. It wasn't as good as a mirror, but it would serve its purpose. I held it up to my face and took a good look at myself. What I saw shocked me more than the date on the newspaper, I had expected to see my hair turned white, wrinkles on my face and sagging cheeks. But what I saw was the way I had looked when I had last looked in a mirror more than twenty years ago. That was impossible! At least that is what I whispered to myself whilst holding the small piece of aluminium and looking at myself in it.*

I hid the small metal piece so that it wouldn't be found and I also kept sneaking peeks through the eyes of Andrew from time to time to keep myself informed of what year it was.

I was given several different projects to work on and I did as well as I could, even though my thoughts were on my image in the piece of metal and the fact that I was now almost eighty years old.

One of the projects that I was given was the attempt to make copies of living organisms. The General called it cloning and he said that this was the future for warfare as we were going to clone a perfect soldier and mass produce him, thus not having to waste 'real' people's lives. But of course I didn't start cloning humans, I started with small animals like rats and mice. One day I managed to clone a sheep, it was the exact copy of the original. Now came the real challenge. I had to clone a human. The General supplied me with some DNA for me to clone. I didn't realise it at the time who it was that I was cloning.

I knew what was to come now. William was the man behind the clone of myself that had attacked me all those years ago. William continued after a short pause.

I recognised the clone that I had created. It was my old friend from my days in Hornet Squadron. I couldn't understand how the General had got hold of that DNA. Once my clone was finished he was taken away from me and I was given another project. One was a colonising project. I was to design deep space vessels that could bring mankind into outer space in order to colonise other worlds. Tied into this project was another one that was called Project Genesis. You have seen results of that project. This forest and all the animals within it were constructed through Genesis. Although now the entire planet has been returned to its former glory through divine intervention. Genesis would have had that effect on the planet if I had have given it enough freedom to spread.

As time went by, I found out that Andrew had been destroyed, well I assumed that he had as I could no longer connect to the cameras he had in his eyes. This was not good news, I was now completely cut off from the rest of the world.

Then the explosion that destroyed the entire planet rocked even my underground laboratory and I realised after some time that probably all life had been made extinct. I found my way through the labyrinthine underground bunker and found an exit at last. I got out of the bunker for the first time in more than a century and got a breath of fresh, albeit arid, air. Well that kind of brings us up to where we are today. Me living in this tavern and serving food and drink to any local survivors. But now that the invaders have been defeated and Earth is back to its truly beautiful self again, I would like to make you an offer that might change your life forever.

Why did I feel like I should say 'Uh oh!'. I didn't of course, but I was starting to feel a bit uneasy as William was starting to act all agitated. I asked him to calm down and tell me what life changing events he had in store for me. He got up from his seat and rushed towards the bar and urged me to follow him.

I think that it will be better, and easier, if I show you what I mean.
Reluctantly I followed. Behind the bar was a door that led into the kitchen. In the kitchen was a trap door. William opened the trap door and walked down the steps. He vanished from sight. I had to make a decision if I was going to follow him or get out of this whole crazy place. But William had been a good friend during the war, and I felt that I owed him a bit more than a doubt, even though he had created both the robot and the clone that had attacked me. I walked over to the trap door and descended into darkness. Soon enough my eyes got used to the darkness and I saw William standing up ahead in a long corridor. He urged me on, and I followed. We walked for what felt like an hour until we came to a steel door. William opened the door and gestured for me to enter. I did and couldn't really make out what was in the room, all I could see was a huge dark shape. Then William turned the lights on in the room and I could see what it was.

Chapter 12

I stood looking at a huge spaceship, not unlike any spaceship from any sci fi movie. I must have looked dumbfounded as William released a loud laugh. *I thought you'd like her. She is the only colony ship that I had time and resources to build. It will do C speed, ah C is of course the speed of light, and will carry Project Genesis and a whole load of worker robots to distant worlds.*

This was all a bit too much for me to digest. Me going into outer-space? Was this a good idea? I still had unfinished work here on earth. Didn't I? My thoughts were racing through my mind as I stared at the spaceship. Finally, a thought struck me, and a decision was made that would change my life forever. I decided that if I did leave Earth then I would have the chance of settling down and living a calm and peaceful life.

I told William that I would join him on the maiden voyage of the spaceship on the premises that I could settle on any planet that I saw fit. William agreed to that, and then started to get everything on board the ship.

A few hours later William and I had everything stored away on board the ship and we were ready to leave Earth behind us.

For those of you that have never had the fortune of travelling into space, I must say that it is an experience that you will never forget. At least the first trip into outer-space will always be lodged in my memory. William was sitting at the controls and was pushing buttons and pulling levers at a speed that I didn't think was possible. The ceiling of the bunker started to open and at the same time the spaceship started to change its position and was being raised from horizontal to vertical. A few seconds later once the ceiling had opened properly the whole ship suddenly came alive. It was vibrating violently, and I was having problems not only speaking and hearing coherently but also thinking coherently. I saw William do thumbs up and before I knew anything else, my stomach went through the soles of my feet and we were heading at breakneck speed away from the ground and towards the outer atmosphere.

It took a few minutes before we had reached a point outside the Earths atmosphere where things levelled off and everything seemed to slow down. I knew for a fact that we were still moving away from Earth at a high speed, although it was having no effect on me at all.

William explained to me that he had created charts of the planets in the solar system and everything that was close by in order for us to be able to plot a course away from here and hit C speed without any fear of flying right through a planet or worse – a sun. He continued explaining that once we hit a part of space that wasn't on his chart, he would use a great tool that he had equipped the ship with. It could scan about 30 light years in any direction and would return within mere minutes giving us information about what is out there. If we found anything, we would head in that direction to investigate, if we didn't then we would head in a random direction for 30 light years and do a new scan. William continued to explain that the tool not only scanned but also mapped the space that was being scanned and fed it into the navigation computer so that we would not have to scan parts of space that we had already been through. A good tool if ever there had been one.

We travelled around for days, perhaps weeks or months, it was hard to tell as time didn't work the same way in space. The scanner finally returned information to us about a solar system about 23 light years from us. We headed in that direction and found a system not too different from our own, the sun was the same colour and size as ours however there were only three planets orbiting it. William scanned the planets for their ability to sustain life and discovered that only the planet furthest away from the sun would be able to sustain any type of life at all. We decided to land on the planet and investigate it.

The surface of the planet was very different from that of Earths, it was rockier and less grassy, and had only small pools of water sporadically placed around here and there. We found a valley that was engulfed in a bowl-shaped mountain formation. It looked ideal for a city. It would be naturally protected from all sides and the only way to reach it would be by the small path that we had walked here on or else by air. The surrounding mountains might even offer something of worth to mine. I told William that this is where I wanted to settle down. He told me that he thought it was a shame to lose my company but that he understood I would like to retire from adventuring. William asked if I would be up for colonists from Earth if the opportunity arose. I thought about it for awhile and finally agreed to it as it would get very lonely here without any human company.

William returned to the ship and flew it to my valley, we unloaded a few boxes from the ship and William commenced to open them up, revealing human-looking robots. When I say human-looking, I mean that they look like humans, without any skin or hair. William started pushing buttons on the back of each robot to activate them and once they were activated, he told the robots that they were to obey me in all my commands. It felt strange but now I was in command of at least four thousand human-looking robots. William smiled at me and said that he would leave first thing in the morning.

Chapter 13

It had taken about three days for all the robots to build a city out of the materials that they had found in some of the other boxes that William had left for me. It was amazing to see them work, they didn't stop to eat or rest, they just kept on working day and night until the city was finished. The next project that I had for the robots was to explore the caverns that surrounded the city. The robots set out to explore and within less than a week all the caverns had been explored and mapped. There were lots of metal and mineral veins in the caverns which would do well for mining. We could either use the raw material to build, or for trading once William started up a regular trade route.

The years went by and the robots lived their everyday lives of working and had even started to enjoy time off to rest and watch TV. They particularly enjoyed watching Robocops and Robot-wars.

In the meantime, I tried to govern Robot City as well as I was able to. The robots obeyed me, and we all got along fine, especially with my personal assistant, a timid robot that went under the name Rowland. I spent many nights discussing everything with Rowland or playing chess. He was a quick learner and evolved in to both a good speaker and a truly magnificent chess player.

Life was good. But as the saying goes, all good things must end. And it did. I am sad to say that the beginning of the end was when William returned for the first time since he had left me here all those years ago. William brought colonists from Earth with him. That was fine of course because it gave me some human company and the robots could learn different things from the new humans that had arrived.

The problems arose some weeks after the first colonists had arrived. The humans felt the robots should not be treated as equals, but should rather be working for the humans. This was not how the robots felt about it, they were used to living their lives the way that they wanted. The humans started picking fights with the robots for the mere satisfaction of causing trouble for them. This was brought to my attention by Rowland and I had to intervene. I addressed the human population and asked them to not cause any more trouble for the robot population. This didn't go down well with the human population and I suddenly found myself a target of hurtling rocks. The humans were in revolt. I needed to put down this revolt as soon as possible and called for assistance from the robots. They answered and soon there were full scale battles going on in the city streets. The robots, which were stronger, managed to round up all the humans and presented them to me. I needed to decide, and it was a very difficult decision, what I should do with them in order to keep the peace. The only thing I could think of was to keep them separated. I ordered the humans to go and live and work in the mines to mine for raw materials and they wouldn't be able to come out until they were willing to live side by side with the robots. The robots marched the humans in front of them into the mines and placed guards outside to keep the humans in. I needed to decide on what to do by the time William would return with more colonists. I set some new laws and in order to maintain them a force of robots were employed. More robots had to be built in order to create this force so it wouldn't create a vacuum in the existence of all the other robots. The human colonists revolted several times in the coming months and were finally subdued in a huge battle. The humans decided that it would be best to remain underground in peace and try make the best of things there. The life underground was not a glorious one, the lack of sunlight catered for pale complexions and larger eyes, as the lack of proper light forced the eyes to evolve in order to pick up the small quantities of light that they had to live with.

The years went by and the humans didn't attempt any more revolts but lived underground, evolving, and prospering as well as they could. The robots continued to live their normal everyday lives and things were looking really good for once. The return of William would once again change all that.
William had brought in more colonists and I had to explain to them that if they wanted to live here, they would have to live underground in the mines. If they didn't accept those terms they would have to get back on the ship and move off somewhere else.

Most of the colonists had paid a lot of money to get a place on the colony ship to this world and could not afford either a return ticket or a ticket to another world. I argued with William and said that he could take them for nothing. He said that he needed the money in order to build more and better ships in the future. I finally had to comply with his request to let the colonists stay. I decided to meet with them all one by one or family by family. Most of the colonists were looking for a new life on a new world and hoping that they wouldn't be too disappointed that I sent them to the mines. One family that I met was going to give me some trouble. They had a small girl of six with them. The only family with a child under eighteen. The laws that had been set all those years ago clearly stated that no children under the age of eighteen would be introduced to the mines. If they were born in the mines it was a whole different matter, but under no circumstances were any children to be taken into the mines. I explained this to the family, and they protested. There biggest issue was what would happen with their daughter. I told them that I would take care of her. I needed to have someone that could clean up my house and my office. She wouldn't be put to work until she reached twelve, up until then she would be given as good an education that I could offer. The parents of the little girl finally gave up their protests and hugged their daughter, kissed her, and then reluctantly left her standing, crying in my office.

I taught little Maggie as much as I could during the first six years until she turned twelve and then I got her to start working for me around the house and the office. She had stopped asking for her parents about three years ago, but she still cried herself to sleep every night. I could hear her all the way from my room. It tore at my heart to hear her and knowing that I had caused her this heartache. But given the circumstances, she would have it better working for me than living and working in the mines. Though she was now only six years away from eighteen and that would mean that she would have to move into the mines according to the laws. Even though I was the one who created the law in the first place, I couldn't make any exceptions, if I did, chaos and anarchy would surely ensue.

When Maggie's 18ᵗʰ birthday was getting closer I felt that I didn't want her to go down into the mines. It wouldn't be right for her to go down there now. Even though she said she still missed her parents, there was no guarantee that they were still alive. But the law stated that she would have to leave the surface when she turned 18. Unless…

I proposed and we got married. That way I got around my own law.

Chapter 14

We had been married for a few years when once again William returned and now things were really going to change.

William told me that Arthur required my return as he was involved in a war that might be much too much for him and the rest of the knights. He needed his Lancelot again. I really didn't want to return to Earth, I really didn't want to leave my world here and my wife. However, I had made a promise to Arthur all those years ago that I would help him whenever he needed my help. I explained to my wife that I was honour-bound to go, but that I would be back as soon as I could. We kissed and I boarded the ship and headed back to Earth. Due to Williams updated ship we were now flying at speeds exceeding five C. William called the engine a Tachyon drive and explained that it wasn't as stable as a normal C drive, however it made us travel five times faster than before, which shortened down any travel time.

I asked William why I was needed this time, the answer I got shocked me. William told me first that Arthur had requested me back to help him out. However, it was the second part of his answer that shocked me. He told me that New Camelot was under siege by a huge army of zombies. That sounded like something from a horror movie. I wondered if I should believe what William was telling me or not. But I knew William and he was not known for lying or exaggerating.

The flight took us only five years instead of twenty-five as it would normally do. And I settled my eyes upon Earth for the first time in about a century. It didn't look as if it had changed much in my absence. It did, however, stir some emotions within me. I hadn't realised until this very moment how much I had missed this blue and green planet.

William brought the ship into Earths atmosphere and plotted a course for Britain and New Camelot. As we approached New Camelot, we flew in over the army that was besieging the huge and beautiful castle. The army was huge and had surrounded Camelot on all sides. I couldn't make out if the army consisted of zombies or not as we were still high up in the air and moving pretty fast. We landed in the courtyard of New Camelot and as we emerged from the ship, we were met by Arthur and some of the knights. They all looked tired and battle-worn.

Lancelot! I'm so glad to see you after so long. Arthur strode up to me and gave me a huge bear hug, I reluctantly hugged him back. *She has been asking for you Lance. She has been asking for you and no one else will do.* I wondered who it was that had been asking for me. My first thought went to Guinevere, had she somehow returned and the whole love triangle would be resurrected along with her. But before my thoughts could evolve any further Arthur continued. *It is my sister Lance. It is Morgana. She is back and she has a huge army of zombies with her. We haven't been able to leave New Camelot in several decades. Luckily, we have farms within the walls, so we are not in dire need of food. However, she has threatened to destroy every single building and kill every single man, woman and child here unless I hand you over.* Why me? What did Morgana want with me? I could understand if she wanted Arthur, but me? I voiced my thoughts to Arthur, and he couldn't give me any satisfactory answer. I knew that I would have to go out and meet her or she would make real her threat to kill everyone here and destroy all New Camelot. I told Arthur that I would go at once to meet her. He urged me not to go, but to join him in a last desperate charge. I laughed a little and said that we wouldn't have a chance as her army was so much larger and consisted of undead beings that would only get up again if they were knocked down. The only way to stop this seemed to be for me to meet up with Morgana and see what she wanted.

I strode over to the huge armoured gates and Arthur ordered them to be opened. The gates opened slowly with a loud creaky noise. I exited through the open gates and walked slowly and proudly towards the army of zombies.

When I approached the zombies, they stepped aside and let me pass. After awhile I reached a small clearing that had three tents in it. I walked towards the largest of the tents and before I reached it, the flap opened, and Morgana stepped out. She smiled a devious smile. *Ah, Lancelot. Welcome to my camp, please enter my humble abode.* Her hand motioned towards the tents opening. I reluctantly entered. Morgana entered close behind. In the tent, I found myself face to face with a man clad entirely in armour from head to toe. His helmet covered his face and I couldn't make out who he was. He started towards me and it looked as if he was about to attack me. *Enough!* Morgana shouted out. I realised she wasn't shouting at me, she was shouting at the armoured man. *I presume you remember my son Mordred.* Then she changed her tune. *Mordred, behave! Lancelot is our guest.* Mordred backed away and sat down on a chair at the far end of the tent. I made sure to keep a watchful eye on him to make sure that he didn't try anything else.

I asked Morgana why she had requested me and not Arthur. Morgana started to laugh. Her laughter rung like a beautiful melody in my ears. She extended her arm towards me and caressed my cheek. I wasn't sure what to make of her actions. She continued to caress my cheek while looking deep into my eyes. Was she trying to hypnotise me? I don't think that she was, but I was starting to feel uncomfortable. She might be an evil woman, but she was also a very attractive evil woman. *I requested you, my dear Lancelot, because out of all the knights, my brother included, you were the man with most passion. Oh, I'm sure that Tristan had passion for Isolde, but your passion for, not only, Guinevere, but for everyone, it surely has no match amongst those stone-cold knights. I need a man of passion, my dear Lancelot. The only way to end this war is by your decision.* Morgana smiled and turned away from me in a seductive move. What was it she wanted from me? *Your silence speaks volumes, my dear Lancelot. But I'm guessing that you want to know exactly how you can put a stop to this war, or should I say siege, as there hasn't been much in the way of battles for the past twenty years. You have two choices really.* Morgana turned to me once again, a smile on her lips. *Your first option is to duel my son, Mordred, to the death. Oh, I know you are both immortals and all that, but that would make it all the more interesting and prolonged, wouldn't you say?* Her smile broadened. *Your second option is,* long pause, *me.* I don't know what she was doing to me, but I wanted her, I knew that I could easily defeat Mordred in a duel and thus end the war, however I wanted her so bad. Had she put a spell on me? I wasn't sure of anything else anymore, only that I wanted her. I motioned towards her and she smiled at me, for me, for only me. She told Mordred to get out of the tent. Then she started towards me, letting her clothes drop to the floor. As she got close to me, she started nibbling my ear and as she was nibbling my ear she started sniffing. Suddenly, she pushed me away. I felt as if I had just woken up from a dream. Had I really wanted her? I think she had had me under some sort of love spell, but it was broken now. *I'm sorry! I didn't know! Please forgive me!* I asked her what she was talking about. *You, you are the one spoken of in the legends and whispered about in the myths.* I had absolutely no idea what she was talking about. *God did not create you!* If not by God, then by whom? What was she talking about? *You are not of God! You are the one of legends, the one of myths! I never foresaw this. This is the third option for ending this war. You win, oh man of legends and myths. I will withdraw my army and lift the siege on New Camelot. You will never be bothered by me again.* I still had no idea what she was talking about, but suddenly Morgana clapped her hands and as soon as she had done that she disappeared and so had also her entire army of zombies along with Mordred. All gone. I didn't know how or why it all had happened and what Morgana meant with calling me the one of legends and myths. It all sounded weird, hadn't I been created by God as everyone else on Earth had? This was a question that I would need an answer for. But how do I get the answer? Tricky question.

I walked back to New Camelot and was met by cheers from everyone there. I didn't feel as if I deserved the cheers that was being heaped upon me. I went to the square where Arthur, William and most of the knights were waiting for me. Arthur started towards me and was about to embrace me until he saw the look on my face. I must have looked pretty scary. My emotions were playing havoc with me due to the things that Morgana had said. Arthur asked what was wrong. I answered that I need to find God. *Don't we all!* Arthur laughed a hearty laugh.

I explained that I wasn't joking, I really needed to find God. No one seemed to know how to do that. William, however, came up with the idea that if we could locate Lucifer, then he would most likely know how to find God. It was a long shot, but worth looking into. The next question was, of course, how would we find Lucifer. Arthur told me that he believed that Sir Gawain had been to hell back in the days when we were all searching for the Holy Grail. Gawain had stumbled accidentally into hell and barely managed to get out. Arthur called for Gawain to come forward. A few moments later Gawain walked up to us, not looking all too excited about having to tell us about his experience in hell. He basically told us the same story that Arthur just had, about how he had been searching for the Holy Grail in a cave and happened to find a gateway into hell itself. He told us of how terrible it was there and how he had problems finding his way out.

I asked him if he remembered where the cave was located. He answered that he remembered that it was on the Welsh coast somewhere but wouldn't tell me exactly where. I grabbed hold of Gawain's chest plate and pulled him roughly towards me. His face was so close to mine that I could smell his foul breath. I growled at him, telling him to take me to the cave and that he had better remember where it is. He snarled at me and released a spray of saliva that hit me in my face. He kept snarling as I repeated my growling question. He snarled and more saliva hit my face. I finished the whole encounter with lifting him off the ground and throwing him across the courtyard. He landed with a loud thudding noise and it took him a few seconds to get to his feet again. There was a large dent in his chest plate from the impact, he looked as if he was gasping for air. I strode quickly over to him and grabbed his chest plate once again and ripped it off his body. Gawain cried out in pain and managed to grab a few breaths of good air before he stood up straight and finally agreed to help me find the gateway to hell.

Chapter 15

We had been searching up and down the entire coast of Wales without any luck in finding the cave. But Gawain was certain that it was here, though after almost two thousand years the geography might have changed a lot. After searching for maybe two weeks, William found a cave that Gawain thought might be the one. We entered and it took us down a winding, slippery path in darkness. William had some torches lit and we continued to walk, winding ever downwards into the belly of this very huge and damp cave. We finally happened upon a huge open area within the cave in which there were hundreds upon hundreds of stalactites and stalagmites. There were also paintings on the walls that bore witness that pre-historic man had inhabited these caves. Gawain exclaimed that this was the cave, he remembered the paintings, these exact paintings. Gawain pointed towards a small crevice in the back part of the cave and said that was were the gate to hell was when he accidentally found it all those centuries ago. I urged us all to go there but Gawain said that he had no wish whatsoever to enter hell, ever again. I didn't argue with him, I would actually be glad to be rid of him. I entered and William followed close behind. Entering the gate was an experience in itself, it felt as if we had just entered a bubble, but that feeling soon dissipated once we were through the gateway. The smell of fire and brimstone, however, was hanging heavily in the air. We walked on in silence, awestruck by our surroundings. The temperature was incredibly high, and I could feel the sweat running down my face, back and on the inside of my thighs. There were eerie sounds coming from the depths further along the stony path that we were walking. If I didn't know any better, I would have said that it sounded like tormented souls. But it couldn't be, could it?

We had been walking for what seemed like ages when the temperature dropped significantly, a cold wind engulfed us and we found ourselves being lifted into the air. After a few seconds of hanging in the air, the cold wind seemed to die down, in its place stood a tall man, whom I recognised from our previous encounter. We were at the mercy of Lucifer. Lucifer suddenly dropped us to the ground. *Oh, it's you! Sorry old chum, if I would have seen that it was you, then I wouldn't have been so forceful. Not a good way to thank a man that saved me from imprisonment. Which by the way, I am very grateful for. Now what brings you and your friend to my domain?*

I told Lucifer the story of how I had met with Morgana and she had told me that I was the one of myth and legend and that I wasn't a creation of God. That I needed to know what she meant and in order to do that I would need to talk with God. I ended my tirade of words with asking Lucifer if he knew how to get in touch with God. Lucifer had looked both bemused and amused during my story and took a long time staring off in the distance before he answered me. *I do know how to get in touch with Yahvew, however are you sure that you want to meet him? If he tells you the truth, are you sure you can handle it?* I told him that I needed to know. He nodded slowly, almost reluctantly and then he gestured for us to follow him. He headed towards a door and we followed him. There was a sign hanging on the door stating that it was a broom closet. Lucifer gestured with his head towards the door. I looked at William and he looked back at me, both of us bewildered. Lucifer gestured at the door with his head again. Neither of us had any idea what he was getting at. Lucifer then yanked the door open and pushed the both of us through it. The sensation when I passed through the doorframe was very similar to the sensation that I had felt when I passed through the portal all those years ago when I had ended up on a different planet and had to fight that lord that was keeping God and Lucifer prisoner. That was a sickening sensation then and this was almost as bad. But the trip was shorter and before I knew it, I was standing in great hall, trying very hard not to let my food return from the way it had once come. William, however, had never experienced travel like this before and wasn't ready for the overwhelming sensation. He left his food in a not so neat pile on the floor. After William had composed himself, I got him to walk with me towards a huge white wooden door. We pushed the door open and came into a room that was almost twice the size of the great hall that we had just come from. On the far side of the room we could see someone standing, looking out of a window. We headed in the person's direction. As we drew closer, I realised that it was Yahvew who was standing at the window. When we had almost reached him, he turned around to face us. He smiled and extended his arms in order to give me a hearty embrace. He held on to me for a good few minutes before letting me go. *My dear friend, how nice to see you again. How can I help the man who saved my life?* I explained to him that I needed to know if he had created me or if he knew who had. He took a step back and took a good look at me. He stood looking me over for a very long time until he finally shook his head. *My dear friend, I will have to retire to my quarter to ponder upon this for some time. Please feel free to wander around here freely. I will get one of my servants to arrange for some quarters for the both of you.* With this said he disappeared out through the huge door. A few minutes later a short, bald man entered the room and said that he was to show us to our rooms. We followed the short, bald man and were soon installed safely in rooms that were created to cater for our every needs.

I rested a few hours on the bed, at least I think it was a few hours, time here seemed somehow different. After getting up I had a nice shower and left my room to go and walk around. I guess it isn't every day that you get to walk around in heaven. I met up with William at a fountain in a big courtyard. He was reading a book titled "The fall of man, who is to blame?" that he had found in the library. I sat myself down next to William on the bench and stretched out my legs in front of me, it was the first time in a long while, not counting the hour or so that I rested on the bed, that I had been able to relax without any worries or concerns. It felt good. No, actually, it felt great. William started reading aloud from the book and I listened for awhile, but soon I found his words grow more and more distant as I drifted off into the land of dreams. But here there didn't seem to be any dreams. I hadn't dreamt when I had the rest earlier, and I didn't dream now either. I just slept and nothing worked its way up through my subconscious to create strange and wonderful scenarios. Dreams didn't seem to exist here for some reason. I was awakened when William had stopped reading the book and had instead shoved me rather hard with his elbow in my side. I was suddenly fully alert and turned to face William with an accusing look. He told me that we needed to find God again and get a straight answer. I said that surely God would come to us when he was done pondering what he needed to ponder about. And besides it hadn't even been more than a day since he said that he needed time to himself. William told me that I shouldn't trust my senses here. We had in fact been here at least three months already. I had difficulties grasping that concept as it surely didn't feel more than a few hours. William stressed the point again that we needed to locate God in order to get the answer that we needed and get out of here. I was inclined to agree with him. We set out to try and find God, but it wasn't an easy task as the domain of heaven was a vast one. After searching for some time, we managed to find one of the short, bald men that seemed to function as servants or helpers to God. We asked the man if he could help us find God, as we really needed to have an answer now and be on our way. The short man asked us to take a seat and wait while he went to fetch God. We sat down on one of the benches next to a beautiful ornate fountain and waited.

Some time later the man returned, with God walking slowly behind him. We asked God if he had any answers for us. He looked upwards for awhile and sighed heavily. *I believe.* He said and trailed off for a moment. *I believe that you are not one of my creations. I am very sure of that. Who created you is something I can't answer at the moment, however I do know someone who should be able to. We need to be off now. We need to go.* He urged us to stand up. *Come! Come with me!* I needed to ask him one more thing before we left, so I asked him what happened when people died. Did they all end up here? *I think you are referring to the afterlife, am I right?* I nodded. *You would be right to think that people who die end up here. At least their souls do. Let me show you before we leave.* God led us away from the fountain and led us through the beautiful garden. We walked for ages until we came to a place that was covered in pure gold. At least it looked like pure gold. *This here is the Golden Field. This is where all good souls end up. Remember that no one is perfect, so I allow for everyone to end up here.* I looked carefully but couldn't see anyone in the Golden Field. *You won't actually see anyone until you yourself die and end up here.* I asked about the screams that we had heard when we went through hell and if they were souls too. *They are indeed souls. Tormented souls. You see not only are we all imperfect, some people are truly evil and commit atrocities in the world. They need to be punished for their deeds and for that, Lucifer was chosen to exact a proper justice upon them. Their screams and moans in hell bear witness to their justified torment. Before we move on, I will tell you about souls. I think it is very important and interesting. I'm sure you will agree with me once you have heard what I have to say on the matter.*

Every living being has a soul. Although humans have often said that animals don't have a soul, I can reassure you that <u>every</u> living being in the entire universe has a soul. You see, the soul is the essence that gives us life, that makes us who we are. When a baby is created copies of the souls from both parents are mixed together in the new vessel, there they call out to a third soul. This soul will most likely be from someone recently deceased who has also been close to either of the parents. There is a network of souls that binds certain souls to each other in thicker bonds than others. The closer a person is with someone else the thicker the bond. Networks can intertwine and mix as people get to know other people, get married, get children of their own, etc. Make sense so far? I nodded, not really understanding everything that he was telling us. *The third soul gets called into the vessel where it meets the copied souls of the parents. The three souls mix together to create a new soul. This new soul is the life essence of the new vessel. You see, as far as I can understand it, souls are beings that live a life without any sensory perception. In their pure form, they can't experience anything. They can't see, smell, hear, feel or taste anything. They need a vessel to do all that for them, hence they inhabit the bodies* *of all living beings in the universe. When a vessel grows old it starts to disintegrate, us immortals excluded of course, the soul will start to prepare to depart. When the vessel ultimately dies, the soul heads into the network of souls, heading home to where souls originate from, but if it is lucky it will be called to mix with two souls in a new vessel. As it leaves the old vessel it creates a copy of itself that is sent either to my realm or Lucifer's depending on if they have been good or bad during their life. The reason for this is that you get the chance to meet your long-lost relatives. There is a lot of comfort in that, and it makes dying a whole lot easier if you can be reunited with your loved ones, or perhaps have a chance at a philosophical discussion with Aristotle. There's more, although I think that will have to wait until another time. We need to go to our intended destination.* And as he said that, he pointed towards a portal. Here we go again!

Chapter 16

I would have thought that after a few of these trips through portals that I would be used to the sensation, but this trip had been much longer than any of the previous ones and I lost what little food I had in my stomach once we arrived at our destination. William, who still wasn't used to these portal trips, was worse off. He was on the ground, curled up in foetus position for a long time, losing all his food and also a lot of stomach acid.

I asked where we were. *We are at the outward station. It was placed here far away from the Golden City, as no one was truly certain that the portal wasn't lethal in any way. We know better now, but of course no one wants to move it.* I needed to re-phrase my question, I needed to know where we were and why. I did my best to ask God the question again. *Oh, I see. We are on the planet of The Overlord. We are here to see if the Overlord has the answers that you seek.* The Overlord? What is going on here? I asked God who this Overlord was. *Ah I should probably tell you this now, however I really need to talk with that man over there first.* God pointed towards a man, clad in a dark green uniform, standing rigid a few metres from us. God went over to the rigid man and spoke softly and quietly. I couldn't make out what they were talking about. After their discussion was over, God returned to us and told us that we needed to get onboard the train once it arrived. In the meantime, he would tell us about the Overlord. *You see, this happened so many thousands of years ago, that it seems impossible to have any bearing on this day and age. But nonetheless it does. The universe was created by an incredibly powerful explosion, caused by a war that the Overlord had been involved in. He decided there and then that there would be no more risks of such major incidents ever again, by creating an army of demi-Gods to watch over the universe. He created an academy on this planet where the demi-Gods trained. I was one of the first, so was Lucifer. We were in the same year and got known for pulling pranks on the others. One of them took bad offence by our pranks, he was Lord Saschka, you know the guy that you defeated on that planet in which I and Lucifer were imprisoned on. Anyway, despite us being pranksters we still managed to graduate as Majors and were allocated a planet to guard over. As we only graduated as Majors we had to share the planet. Anyone who graduated as a Colonel or higher where allocated a planet on their own. We got Earth, at the time a lifeless planet with no personality at all. We changed all that. We created the one-celled organisms, that slowly evolved into the different life forms that inhabited Earth.*

The train arrived and we got on. God continued his story, as the train sped off towards the Golden City.

Anyway, to continue, The Overlord is our superior officer and despite never meeting him in the flesh, I'm sure that he will grant us an audience. Anyway, as I was saying, the reason I believe that he will know the answers to your questions is that there are certain myths and legends surrounding the Overlord, that if they are true then you will certainly have all the answers that you need.

I must confess, that everything that I was being told confused me. The train sped on through a mountainous terrain and soon I could see The Golden City growing as we got closer. I could now see why it was called The Golden City. The entire city gleamed as if it had been built up entirely of gold. Towering over all the other buildings was a majestic, golden castle. I guessed that this was the home of the Overlord. The train entered The Golden City via an underground tunnel, and suddenly came to a jarring halt at a station. We exited the train and a guard ushered us towards a lift. The lift brought us directly up to the golden castle that I had seen from a distance earlier, or at least up to the gates. Outside the large gates stood two guards. They were both armed with poleaxes, which looked incredibly menacing. In fact, the guards looked really intimidating, but I guess guards need to look that way in order to keep unwanted people from entering the gates. Yahweh went up to the guards and introduced himself. The guards straightened themselves up even more, if possible, and saluted him. One of the guards shouted out an order to open the gates, to someone that we couldn't see. With a loud clanking noise, the two gates started to part from each other, and we could soon enter the castle. The interior of the castle was as golden as the exterior. I had never in my life seen anything like it, and that is saying a lot as I had seen a lot of wonders back on Earth. But this wasn't Earth, this was another planet altogether, the planet of the Overlord. Not only was the interior golden, the walls and ceilings were adorned with beautiful paintings of different sceneries and people. I walked down the hallway, looking at all the paintings, but I wasn't able to see all of them. Even if I would have stayed in in this place for several weeks, I might still not manage to see all the paintings. But walking past them made it impossible to see more than a few of them. Because I wasn't looking where we were going, I didn't notice that we had reached a large door, until I walked right into it. I rubbed my nose, which had taken the full brunt of the door, and turned ashamedly to Yahweh and William who were trying very hard not to laugh. Yahweh knocked on the door and within a few seconds it opened. As I entered through the door my senses were overwhelmed. The room that we were in was clearly the throne room of the Overlord, I could see him in the far end of the room, although the room was so huge that he didn't appear to be larger than an ant. The room, as I mentioned earlier, was huge, it was also golden and adorned with paintings all over the walls and ceiling. There were several long tables standing in rows which took up most of the floor. Happy and cheerful people were sitting at the tables, eating, and drinking merrily, oblivious to us new-comers. We walked past all the happy people, making our way to the throne and the Overlord. As we came within a proximity of the Overlord, two guards barred our way with their poleaxes. Again, Yahweh introduced himself, although these guards didn't seem impressed. Yahweh told them that he needed to speak with the Overlord, that it was very important. He then made a gesture towards me with his hand. The guards took one look at me and their eyes grew wide and their jaws dropped. They looked at each other then back at me. *He can go, but you and the other one need to stay here.* The guard had pointed at me when he said that. They parted their poleaxes and motioned me to come forward. Yahweh gave me a nudge as I had apparently been hesitating. I passed the guards and made my way to the throne. The Overlord seemed oblivious to my approach, or so I thought, but suddenly he got up and ordered me to stop and come no further. I stopped in my tracks waiting for whatever was going to happen next. The Overlord was looking at me, when he suddenly jumped down from the dais, on which his throne was situated, and walked towards me with great strides. As he came closer, I could see what he looked like.

Here is the freaky part: He. Looked. Like. Me!

My jaw dropped. The Overlord stopped in front of me. It felt like I was looking in a mirror. Was the Overlord a clone of me? Was I a clone of the Overlord?

The Overlord didn't say anything for a few minutes, he just stood and stared at me. Then he cracked a smile and started to laugh. *It is you!* He said with glee in his voice. *Don't you remember me?* I can't say that I did remember him. As far as I knew, I had never met him before, unless he was the clone of me that I had fought on Earth. I remained silent, not sure of what I should say. *Brother! Don't you remember me, your own brother?* Brother? My brother? I told him that I didn't remember ever having a brother. *Do you have a huge scar on your head?* What an odd question, why would I have a scar on my head? I was immortal, my wounds healed immediately by themselves, leaving no scars. I shook my head. *Let me see!* Before I could object, he started examining my head, pulling my hair aside. *Aha! There it is, can you feel it?* He took my hand and placed it on a part of my head. I felt something there, it felt strange, almost like a… scar! But that was impossible. Wasn't it? How could I have a scar? As if reading my mind, the Overlord said: *An arrow pierced your skull, it was made from xth metal, the only element that can truly cause us harm.* With that, the Overlord embraced me. When he let me go, he looked at me again, with a warm smile. *I guess your wound may have done some damage to your memory. Come, sit down and I will tell you your story, perhaps that will trigger your memories to return.* He gestured for me to come over to the throne and sit down next to him. *There were three of us in the beginning, well three brothers at least. We were princes. Our father was the King, probably still is. Life was pretty simple and peaceful. We would spend our days riding our Sleipners, reading books, wooing women, fishing, philosophising and so much more. There was you: Avalon, me: Avatar, and our youngest brother: Boris. The three princes that lived the life. That was before the prophecy. The prophecy changed everything.* The Overlord, Avatar, suddenly looked very sad. *The prophecy...* He lingered a long time on this word and would repeat it several times before continuing again. *The prophecy was our downfall. Our undoing. There had been large letters written in flames on the side of one of our greatest mountains, Mount Aedelbra, that spelt out something awful, something so terrible that it haunts me to this day. The words that had suddenly appeared on the mountain said: "The father, the King, will die by the hands of his Son." Nothing more than that! Nothing more was needed. Our father took the words seriously. One of his sons was going to kill him. That is when our father, Arton, started to scheme and plan our deaths. At least your death, perhaps he wanted you out of the way first because you were the oldest of us. Not that age ever matters for someone that can live for eternity. Three times he attempted to have you killed. It was during the third attempt that you got the wound that has left you with that scar.* Without thinking about it, I reached up to my head to feel the scar. *You had been out riding on your favourite Sleipner out by the waterfalls of R'has, your favourite place for riding and reading, not to mention dating. But this day was different. Someone was waiting for you. Someone who was armed with a bow and arrow. Arrows that were made from the xth metal. The arrow was fired as you rode close to the waterfalls of R'has and pierced your skull. You fell off your Sleipner and into the river. The current dragged you towards the waterfall and you went over it. I believe that fall was your salvation. If you would have remained in the same place where you had fallen off your Sleipner, the assassin would have finished off the job. Luckily the river swept you away and some farmers found you further down the river. They sent word to Boris who came and brought you back* to the castle. *We took turns standing watch over you to make sure that no further attempts to kill you were made. Word of your state reached the nobles and the people, most of them supported us, but there were some who were loyal to the King, and wouldn't believe that he would be behind an attack on his own son. Lines were drawn, sides were taken, and battles commenced. When we found out about what was going on outside the castle, we decided that we needed to come up with a plan on how to save your life. Boris suggested that he smuggle you off planet and go in to hiding until you were fully restored. Then you'd both return and challenge our father. As neither of you ever returned, I figured that you were both lost, or dead. The ship that Boris was using to get you off planet was rapidly followed by three Darkspear fighters. That was why I feared the worst. I couldn't wait around much longer, I had to get off the planet too. I feared that father would try and have me killed too. I gathered together a group of people that were loyal to me. A lot of our loyalists had been imprisoned on Arkhanoid, but there were still enough of them free and willing to follow me to freedom. We fled the planet and ended up here, where I started to build up an empire with guardians that would stand guard against any attempts that our father would do on attacking us. It started out on a small scale. There weren't that many of us initially, but over time children were born and grew up. I designed The Academy to train up Guardians to safeguard the universe. It was a long and arduous task, especially sending every Guardian to their designated planets. The trips there took centuries. But once they arrived, they set up the portals that would lead back to here. That way travel was significantly shortened. But never in my dreams would I have guessed that you were on one of the planets under my protection. Where is Boris? I would have thought he would have been with you?*

I shook my head. *I can't remember neither you nor Boris. I can tell you what my first memories are of. If you have the time.* My brother nodded.

I remember waking up. I was lying on the ground. I remember a swamp. I remember some trees. I remember the wildlife. Huge and ferocious creatures, small and ferocious creatures, huge and docile creatures, and a whole deal more of various sizes and ferocity. In the future, these creatures would become known as Dinosaurs. Every day was a battle for survival. There were hundreds, if not thousands of dinosaurs that were hunting for meat and they didn't mind if I was on the menu. Not even the plant-eating dinosaurs were safe to be around. Some were so large that they couldn't see me, which meant that I had to dodge their huge feet as they came thundering down to earth. Some plant-eating dinosaurs weren't so huge, but they had evolved defensive armour and offensive weapons like spiky tails or spiky horns to fend off any meat-eating dinosaurs, or yours truly. As I mentioned before, every day was a battle for survival, but I did survive and against all odds too. The next part is a difficult part to speak about, as I don't really know what actually happened, it is basically my memory of the event, although it might be mixed up with the popular scientific theory of what had happened. I remember a star growing in size. I remember it hitting Earth somewhere far away over the horizon. I remember that the sky lit up in orange and red. I remember seeing the dinosaurs flee away from that direction in panic. I remember running too. I remember thinking that this would be the day that I would die. I didn't die, although it was a close call several times. Dinosaurs were stampeding, I almost got crushed beneath their gigantic feet on more than one occasion. A huge cloud of smoke covered the sky and shut out the sun. That was the beginning of the end for those gigantic creatures. First there were horrendous storms of fire that swept in after us as we fled in the opposite direction. Once the fires died out it got cold. Really, really cold. The dinosaurs couldn't handle the immense drop in temperature and started dying. I remember it clearly as I realised that I wouldn't have to go hungry. But other meat-eating scavengers had the same idea, and I found myself competing for the abundant food with small, furry rodents.

Once the dead dinosaurs started to rot a new age of suffering and starvation began. The small furry rodents started to evolve in to larger and larger animals in order to stay on top of the food game.

If you were small you were likely to be eaten, if you were large you were more likely to survive. I held my own against the gigantic meat-eating animals. But as the dinosaurs had both carnivores and herbivores, so did the furry animals, in later days identified as mammals. They never achieved the same size as the now extinct dinosaurs, but they were truly huge and majestic, and dangerous. I can't say how it happened, because I really have no idea. Suddenly there were furry animals that walked on two legs. They were mostly short and resembled the apes that lived in the jungle, although different in some ways. They could use simple tools. I kept my distance from them as they showed fear of me whenever I came close to their homes. I must have been a very strange sight to them. A fur-less creature that towered over them. For their own sake, I kept my distance. Although there were times that I wished that I could go to their camp and get to know them. Just for the company. That was something that bothered me, although I didn't really know of it at the time what it was. I felt alone, later on in life I would realise this. As the small bipedal, furry animals evolved in both size and skills with tools and hunting, they started to take a different approach to me. They didn't seem to be frightened of me anymore, just curious. I would often sit high up on a rock and enjoy the sun beating down on my face. Even with my eyes closed I could sense these animals getting closer, then they would stop and just look at me for what seemed like a very long time. Then they would leave. And that is how it kept on, day after day, week after week, month after month, year after year. Although I had no notion of these measurements of time back then.

As time went by, I noticed more and more difference in these animals. They were not so furry anymore, the structure of their skulls became different, their hands, their feet, their entire posture had changed. It was around this time that I noticed that they were trying to communicate with me. I didn't realise it at first, but one day as some very courageous animals – no I can no longer call them that – perhaps I should call them pre-humans – any way some very courageous pre-humans approached my cave where I had lived for several years. They entered the cave, cautiously.

Then sat down in front of me. They didn't seem hostile or scared of me. They sat in the dimly lit cave, and at first I thought they were just sitting there, fidgeting. They were moving their hands in strange ways. But after a while I realised, they weren't fidgeting. They were trying to talk to me using their hands. If only I could understand what they were trying to tell me.

It took many attempts and a lot of pointing at objects and repeating certain hand gestures before we were all making ourselves understood. It was a great feeling. I suddenly felt as if I was a part of something, not just a someone that stood on the outside of the group looking in. It was a new beginning for me, and for them. It took some more time before their entire clan welcomed me in. But I never gave up and neither did those intrepid few that had dared enter my cave in the first place. Soon I was sitting with the entire clan, talking with them with my hands. I think this was the first time that I came to realise that others grew old and died, but I remained the same. Time after time people that I cared for, grew older and died. And time after time my heart broke and I still didn't understand why I didn't' grow old and die too. I paused for a while to fight back the tears that were starting to build up in my eyes.

Time went on and the clan members grew older and died, new children were born, and it appeared to me that this was just the normal cycle of life, but I wasn't part of it. I was something else, even though I didn't know what I was.

Then one day, don't ask me how they came into being or where they came from, as I have no idea, but there they were all the same, people that resembled me more than anyone in the clan. Were they like me? That was my question. It was also the question of my family, the clan. They had all grown up with me, I was part of their family, their clan. But I wasn't like them in appearance. These new people, they stood tall, they didn't have much in the way of hair either. Just like me. Just like me. The clan had a meeting with me, and we discussed me and my future with them or with the new people, that might be mine. That were most probably mine. It was with heavy hearts they decided it best that I leave them and

join with the new people. It was with a heavy heart that I agreed
with them, and again that was the end of an era for me and the
beginning of a new one. These people not only resembled me, they
were also very clever with inventing new tools when needed.
I guess time moved on again. I lived with these new people and
learnt how to use words to make myself understood. I knew,
somewhere in the back of my head that I had been able to use
words before, but I hadn't used any for so long that I didn't know
how anymore. I was learning it all again, fresh from the start. But
it was refreshing, I guess it must be like how a child feels when
they learn how to speak for the first time in their lives. I soon
learnt the language of several tribes. Every so often the different
tribes would meet up in huge trade-meets, there they would trade
anything and everything, including ideas and women. I figured that
the exchange of women meant that they could keep the bloodlines
free of the taint of incestual elements. That had not been the case
with the clan that I had lived with previously. They hadn't bothered
if they mated with someone they were related to, as long as it
wasn't their direct relative.
Time did move on, and I remained the only constant in the tribe,
everyone else grew old and died. I become something of a
peculiarity amongst the different, neighbouring tribes. People
would come from long distances away just to see me and exchange
a few words. Some people would just stand and stare at me, some
would dare to walk up to me and touch me to make sure that I was
indeed alive. My name became Man-with-long-life and it was true,
I was a man with a long life. A very, very long life. I often
wondered why I didn't grow old and die. I never reached any
answer, neither did anyone else. Not even the Shaman of the tribe,
who was very attuned with the spirit world, had an answer for me.
He only knew that I wasn't a spirit, anything else about me was
beyond him.
Time passed by and the tribe started to grow. Soon we were so
many that we had to start to re-plan the structure of our village.
Over time the village grew and grew, so did our neighbours, and
there were rumours of a huge tribe forming across the sea. The

rumours said that they called themselves Sumerians and were gathering neighbouring tribes to form something that they called an Empire. It was supposed to help protect them against any incursions by wandering nomads. I thought this sounded fascinating and decided it would be worth paying a visit to this Sumerian Empire. A few other men of my tribe also thought it sounded like a good idea. Early one spring day, fifteen of us set out on a trip that would take us the furthest away from our tribe that we had ever been, although now in retrospect I had already travelled across the vast universe, but of course I wasn't aware of this at the time. It took us all the way to the summer to reach the Sumerian border. When we reached the border, men armed with spears stopped us. They asked us what our business was. When we told them that we were just curious about the whole concept of the Empire, they conferred amongst each other, then agreed to let us travel through their lands as long as we didn't cause any trouble. Causing trouble wasn't our intention, so we travelled along the small and dirty tracks until we reached a huge village. It was in fact not a village at all, but rather something they called city. High walls surrounded the city, made of a material that we weren't accustomed with. We truly felt out of place here as we walked around in awe of everything that we could see, we really didn't know where to look as the whole place was so huge and there were so many people in the streets. I couldn't be sure, but it felt like there were more people here than there had ever been in one of the trade meetings of the tribes back home. No, I was more than sure that there were more people here in this city than there were in all the neighbouring tribes back home. It was mind-boggling. We continued walking down the streets of the city, looking at everything and everyone until we entered a huge open area, which was filled with even more people and they seemed to be selling all sorts of things, from grain to donkeys, and things that we had never seen before. It truly was an amazing, and at the same time terrifying sight. As we didn't have anything of our own to trade with, all we could do was walk around and look at the wares that were available. Day soon turned to dusk, and we had to find some place to stay for the night. As we didn't have anything of value to pay with, finding a place to stay proved to be very difficult. The Sumerians seemed to use small, round discs of a metal they called bronze and the discs they called coins. On each coin was etched a picture of some kind of deity that they worshipped, each coin seemed to have a different deity etched on it. But we didn't have any. At last we reached a small house in which lived an old man. We told him our story and that we didn't own any of the strange metal discs that people here seemed to use to trade with. He laughed at us, not in a nasty way, but in a kind of understanding way, he then bade us enter his house to spend the night there. He offered us food and drink and we talked for a long time until it was time for all of us to get some sleep. The next morning the man asked us if we would be willing to do some work for him in exchange for some bronze coins. We all agreed, as that would make our life here in the city so much easier. We chopped wood for the fire, went out to the market to buy food and other wares that the old man needed, we cooked, cleaned his house and even scrubbed the outside of his house until it was shiny white. For all this the man gave us fifteen bronze coins and an offer to let us stay for as long as we wanted in exchange for more work and more bronze coins. I think at that point we were all hooked on the prospect of earning more of these bronze coins. It seemed such an easy trade commodity, imagine not having to lug a huge animal, or sack of grain to trade for something else, just carry around these small pieces of bronze until you see what you want and then use them to trade with. Wonderful!

So, life went on in the Sumerian capital and days turned to weeks, weeks turned to months, and months had suddenly turned to several years. We were happy working for the old man, whose name was Ibrahim, but my friends were all growing old and weak and soon they departed their lives. Ibrahim, who had been pretty old when I got to know him, was still alive, although he looked even older than before. One day Ibrahim told me that he had had a visitation from God. I asked him which God, and he laughed at me. He told me there was only one God. This was a strange concept to *me as I had always been aware of many Gods. They existed in every living thing and helped fend off evil spirits. The idea of there being only one God was new to me and I asked Ibrahim to tell me more. He told me that God had created Earth in six days and rested on the seventh. God had created the oceans, the rivers, the land, the skies, the sun, all the animals and finally God had created humans. God was everywhere, saw and heard everything. God was almighty, powerful, merciful, however would swiftly punish any injustice that was done. Ibrahim continued to tell me that God had told him to take all his belongings and move in the direction of the setting sun, until he reached what had been described as the promised land. Ibrahim then asked me to go fetch his wife, who lived in another part of the city. I was taken aback, after all these years living and working with Ibrahim, not once had he mentioned that he had a wife. He told me that married couples are taxed very highly and therefore they had decided to live apart from each other. He said that he would finish packing up all his and my stuff, then meet me at the western oasis at dusk this evening. I went to find the house in which Ibrahim's wife, Sarai lived. He hadn't been wrong, it was truly in a different part of the city, in fact it was as far away from his house as you could venture. I knocked on the door of the house that Ibrahim had described to me. An old woman opened the door and inquired who I was and what I wanted. When I told her about her husband and leaving the city to head to the promised land, I expected her to scoff at the whole idea, however her whole face lit up and she asked me to help her get all her belongings together. The belongings included not only clothes and furniture, but a whole household of people who were unfree. They were called slaves and had to work for no money at all. I thought this very odd as I thought everyone here worked for the bronze coins. When I asked Sarai about the slaves, she laughed and said that almost everyone in the city had slaves to help them do work. I then asked where these slaves came from. I was told that most of the slaves were the spoils of wars with other tribes, others had been sold into slavery by their parents as the parents had been very poor and needed coins. I decided that I* didn't like the whole concept of slavery, no one should work for nothing, it was wrong, especially as the slaves were also marked with tattoos on their face to show that they were property.

It was almost dusk by the time everything had been loaded up into carts. Huge oxen pulled the carts as we headed to exit the city and rendezvous with Ibrahim at the western oasis. When we reached the oasis, Ibrahim was already waiting for us, so was his nephew, Lot. There were also thousands of sheep, goats and more than a few donkeys.

We spent the night at the western oasis before heading out at dawn. When we set out it was nothing like when I left my old tribe with my friends. We had left on foot with only the fur-skins on our backs, but now it was more like a gigantic exodus of people moving in a long caravan. The noise and smell from the animals, was more than enough to drive me crazy, but before long I seemed to get used to both.

The road to the promised land was long and full of bandits and wild animals. I did my best to protect the whole cortège from both the bandits and the wild animals. By the time we reached the promised land, Canaan, there was a famine and there was no way that we would be able to survive on the meagre yield of the land. Dismayed Ibrahim decided to continue westward. We crossed over a desert and entered a land that we soon found out was called Egypt and was ruled by a Demi-God that the people called Pharaoh.

Ibrahim needed to plea with the Pharaoh in order to give us some land to settle on, but the Pharaoh took a liking to Sarai and asked if she was Ibrahim's wife. Ibrahim, fearing that he would be killed if he said that she was, told the Pharaoh that Sarai was his sister. The Pharaoh gave Ibrahim, not only land, slaves and jewellery in exchange for Sarai.

I didn't agree with what Ibrahim had done, but I held my tongue as I only worked for him and wasn't his equal, at least not according to Ibrahim himself.

We hadn't been on our new land very long before Sarai broke down and told the truth to the Pharaoh, who become enraged and *forced us off the land and out of Egypt. We returned to Canaan, the promised land, and now the famine was over, and the land was brimming with life, and food was suddenly plentiful. We settled down on a good patch of land and things seemed joyous for everyone, including the slaves. Although food was now in abundance, Lot decided that he would try his luck away from his brother, so he left with all his family, slaves, and animals to settle in a different part of the promised land. Lot and his family settled in the city of Sodom, which in hindsight was a huge mistake. Lot hadn't been in Sodom very long when the city was sacked by Chedorlaomer, King of Elam, and Lot and his family were taken as slaves. When Ibrahim heard of this, he gathered together the rest of the family and put me in charge of a huge force that would go and rescue Lot. We attacked at night and the King of Elam, and the three other kings that he had allied himself with, fled from us in terror. Ibrahim ordered us to follow them to end their miserable lives once and for all. The terrible deed was carried out close to the city of Damascus.*

It was not long after this that Ibrahim claimed that God had spoken with him again and foretold him that in the future his people would be living as slaves in Egypt, until a leader of men would lead them out of the land of the Pharaoh, across the Red sea, through the desert and back to the promised land again. As Ibrahim's wife was barren, it seemed as if Ibrahim's line would end with him and there would be no people of Ibrahim to become slaves in Egypt or be led to freedom. It was then that Ibrahim's wife Sarai came up with the plan of giving one of her hand-maidens to her husband, so that the prophecy would have a chance of coming true. The hand-maiden, Hagar, soon bore a child, however animosity between Hagar and Sarai soon became so bad that Hagar was forced to flee. Not long after Hagar had fled, did she return, claiming that a messenger of God had told her to return and make peace. She was going to have a son, and he was going to be called Ishmael.

Many years later when Ibrahim was almost 100 years old, Ibrahim claimed that God had spoken with him again, telling him to change

his name to Abraham, meaning Father of many nations, and he
was to start circumcising boys and men as a sign of faith and a
kind of contract with God. Abraham was also told that his wife
Sarai, who would now be called Sarah, was to bear him a son.
This was hard to believe, considering their high age and the fact
that Sarah was barren.

But I guess miracles do happen. Sarah became with child. But
before this happened, something weird and pretty scary occurred.
Three strangers arrived and spent some time in Abraham's tent.
What was discussed in there I have no idea, but after many hours
in the tent, the three strangers and Abraham left the tent and went
up a hill that overlooked Sodom. Again the three strangers and
Abraham were discussing unheard by my ears. Soon after, the
strangers departed for Sodom. Night fell and I was wandering
about, unable to sleep. Something was eating away at my mind, I
didn't know what, but something was wrong, something was going
to happen. I stopped at the top of the hill where, just hours ago,
Abraham and the three strangers had stood. I looked out over the
sinful town of Sodom, when all of a sudden the black sky lit up like
a furnace. There was a huge fiery blast that came down from the
sky and incinerated Sodom. I was shocked, and scared. What could
have caused that? A part of me thought that it might be the God
that Abraham had made a contract with, although a part of me just
didn't want to believe that. A part of me wanted to find a rational
answer, something that made more sense than the wrathful hand of
God sending fire from the sky. It was at this point I made my
decision to leave. If Abraham had such power at his disposal, I
didn't want to be a part of it. I made my way to Egypt again, to see
if I could secure a position in the court of the Pharao.

Suddenly my story was interrupted by a servant running towards
us. The servant ran up to us and stopped mere inches away from
us. He handed my brother a rolled up and sealed piece of paper.
My brother broke the seal and unrolled the paper, then he let his
eyes wander upon the words.

My brother told me that the message was of no direct importance, took out a clear piece of paper, scribbled a few words on it, rolled it up and took out his seal and wax from his pocket to seal the response. He handed the rolled up piece of paper to the messenger, who rapidly ran off.

My brother asked me what I intended to do. I told him that I would like to go see my father, just to find out if things were better and if so try and reconcile the family again. My brother didn't think it was a good idea, however he wasn't going to stand in my way if that was what I wanted to do.

I think you are making a huge mistake. I told him that it didn't matter, I needed to go back to see if my memories would return. My brother nodded solemnly and understandingly. *You will need to hitch a ride to get there. Not many ships have sufficient licences to travel into The Inner Circle. I'll send out a message to all Merchant ships to see if anyone has a licence and is en route to The Inner Circle. It might take some time though. In the meantime, please make yourself at home. Do you mind if I use your friend, William's expertise with building ships?* I told him I didn't mind, as long as William didn't. *Then that is a deal. Until a Merchant ship heading to The Inner Circle arrives, you are to stay here and enjoy yourself, and your friend, if he agrees, will help me design a new fleet. I have a feeling that we will be needing one soon, if things go bad with your visit with father.*

Chapter 17

The days went by, which turned in to weeks, then months. That is by this planets' standards at least. No idea how that would measure by Earth standards, but I seemed to fill my time by sparring with my brother, wandering around the beautiful Palace gardens, perusing through the many art galleries and libraries, meeting up with people and discussing everything and nothing at all. It was almost as if I had finally managed to find peace in my life. Peace at last, and what was it I wanted to do? I wanted to go and find my father, a man that had, according to my brother, tried to have me killed on more than one occasion. Was I crazy? Probably! I should just stay here and become part of this peaceful life. But I needed to know. I needed to know the truth. I wanted to be able to remember my life, as it had been, before Earth, back on my planet, with my father and two brothers. I didn't have my memories, all I had was a story that my brother had told me. What if my father told me another story of what had happened? Who should I believe? I couldn't trust my own memories, as I didn't have any from that time. But still, I wasn't even sure that I could make it there. According to my brother, only certain Merchant ships were allowed to travel into The Inner Circle. So far, there had been no response to the message he had sent out. I had almost given up hope. Then one day, a message was received from a Merchant ship called The Hermitage Shanks. It was going to arrive within the next few days and was then due to head into The Inner Circle. My brother delivered the message to me himself, while I was sitting on a bench enjoying the scenery of the beautiful Palace gardens. Did I mention how beautiful the Palace gardens were?

My ticket to go and be reunited with my father was just days away. I felt excited and nervous. What if he would try and kill me again. It would appear that he might have the means to do it, if my head-wound was anything to go by.

The Hermitage Shanks had arrived. I was escorted to its landing bay by my brother, William and a few of my brother's bodyguards. The area where ships landed was particularly rough, so my brother wasn't taking any chances.

As we entered the landing bay, I laid eyes upon the ugliest spaceship in creation. It was so ugly that it reminded me of a toilet. The name of the ship, Hermitage Shanks, was painted in large orange-coloured letters on the upper part of the ship. There were three people standing outside the ship. I guessed that it was the crew. My brother led me up to them and started the introductions. *Gentlemen, this here is my brother, Avalon, or as he is better known now, James. This is his friend, William. James, William, meet the crew of The Hermitage Shanks: This is Captain Flush Jordan* (The captain nodded his head to us), *this is Science Officer Shanks* (The Science officer waved a happy wave), *and this is Navigation Officer Hermitage* (The Navigation officer didn't acknowledge us, instead he continued chewing on whatever it was that he was chewing on). *Captain Flush, can you get my brother through the blockade and into The Inner Circle?* The Captain nodded. *Excellent, it is settled. Avalon, you will travel with Captain Flush and his crew, they will drop you off on the only planet within The Inner Circle that is inhabited, that is where you will find our father. Best of luck!* Avatar hugged me, then turned and walked away.

The Captain motioned for us to come aboard his ship. I couldn't help but think, if this ship was safe to fly in.

I got to sit up in the Bridge with the Captain, and at first, he didn't say much. He was pretty busy getting the ship ready for take-off, then manoeuvring away from the gigantic planet's atmosphere. Once we were free of the planet, it was a different matter altogether. It turned out that Flush and his crew were from Earth and had fought in the Uranian war. I told him that I had never heard of that war. Flush laughed and then said that he would tell me why I had never heard of the war. He would tell me the story of The Hermitage Shanks.

You see, it all started many years ago. I was a fighter pilot in Spar Fleet. I was the best of the best. Every other pilot wanted to either be me or kill me so they could be the best of the best. All the women wanted me. Life was good. I enjoyed being popular. But things were happening outside of my control. Decisions were being made that I didn't have a clue about. Things that would change my life forever. After another successful mission against the Uranians I was called in to my Commanding Officer's office. Strange thing with wars, they are sometimes fought over stupid things. This war was fought over a really stupid thing. You see, when we first sent manned spaceships to Uranus, we discovered that the planet was inhabited. They weren't humanoids mind you, they were more like gelatinous blobs with eyes on stalks. But all the same they were not only sentient, but also pretty intelligent. Everything seemed to be going really well. until they found out that we called them Uranians. They objected to this vehemently and it went so far that they declared war on all humans. I interrupted Flush's story by asking what they had wanted to be called. Flush laughed. *They wanted to be called by their proper name which was Urectums. And for this we went to war. A war that lasted decades and saw hundreds of thousands die on both sides. Anyway, I digress, as I was saying I was called in to the office of my Commanding Officer. What he told me was going to change my life forever, in ways that I would never have been able to foresee. He invited me into his office. Colonel Oon was sitting behind his desk as I entered. He made an inviting gesture with his hand towards one of the chairs that were situated in front of his desk. I sat down.*
He then went about telling me that I had become too popular, too good at what I did, that everyone else felt inadequate in relation to me, and intimidated by me. I started to protest, but he quickly shut me up with another gesture of his hand. He continued to tell me that he had orders from high command to make me a Captain of a patrol ship. A patrol ship that was supposed to patrol the inner four planets of the solar system. I knew what that meant. I wouldn't see any action again. The inner four planets consisted of Mercury,

*Venus, Earth and Mars, and had not been touched by the war so
far. None of the Uranians ships had the capacity of travelling that
far, yet. But being put in charge of a patrol ship and end up
patrolling that area was a bad career move. But it seemed as if I
didn't have much choice in the matter. I was to report to General
Ifo at Spar Fleet command and await transport to my new patrol
ship, The Hermitage Shanks.*

*I was told that The Hermitage Shanks was a new, state of the art
Patrol ship and the crew were top-notch, best of the best, and all
that. I almost felt cheerful for a few moments at the prospect of
working with others of my calibre. Boy was I heading for
disappointment.*

*After arriving at Spar Fleet command and meeting with General
Ifo, I was ushered away to the hangar where The Hermitage
Shanks was waiting for me. You can probably imagine my
disappointment when I set eyes upon it. Go on, admit it, you must
have had similar thoughts when you saw it. But don't let its looks
deceive you, it is a whole lot more than what it seems. But I'll get
to that part in a while.*

*I went aboard and hoped to meet the rest of the crew, but there
was no one to be found. I went to the bridge to get myself
acquainted with the controls of the ship. I had only flown one-
person fighter ships previously, so getting to grips with how a ship
like this would fly was going to be a challenge for me. But I wasn't
going to let it defeat me. I wasn't going to let Colonel Oon and the
others from Spar Fleet get the better of me. I would show them that
Flush Jordan will survive this tedious mission and return to the
war and finish it off single-handedly. Then I would seek out
revenge on Oon and the others for this humiliation. Ah yes, my
plan for revenge was a good one. But other matters came in the
way, as I will soon tell you about.*

*I had been on the ship for some time, getting to know the controls,
when there was a knock on the door. I shouted out "Enter" and the
sliding door opened up and two men walked into the Bridge. One
man was short, with long, greasy brown hair, the other one was of
medium height and looked as if someone had cut his hair using a*

bowl. The short man introduced himself as Hermitage. His voice was low and drawling. It made him sound like he wasn't all that bright. He continued to tell me that he was the Navigation Officer. I remarked that it was a strange coincidence that he was called Hermitage, as that was also part of the ship's name. The second man then introduced himself as Shanks, the Science Officer. He had a shrill voice and tended to stutter a bit when he talked, as if he was constantly nervous. Again, I remarked on the coincidence of the name, but then thought there might be something else behind the names, but I decided to let it go for the time being.

We hadn't been on the ship for more than a few days when the following incident occurred, and I can tell you, this part will send chills down your spine.

I had entered the living quarters, wanting to read the J.E.P. however I soon realised that someone else had beaten me to it. My money was on that greasy little Hermitage. I called out for him but got no reply. I called again, still no reply. After a third attempt, the door to the living quarters opened and Hermitage came walking in, holding a plate of Swedish meatballs in one hand and greedily stuffing his face with the said meatballs with his other hand. "Wassup?" was his greeting. I asked him directly if he had read my newspaper, he told me he hadn't. He then told me, in his low drawl, that he couldn't read. I wasn't at all surprised about that. He then told me that, even if he had been able to read, he wouldn't have read something so trashy as the J.E.P! I was aghast! I told him that there was absolutely nothing wrong with The Jupiter Evening Post. But he wouldn't listen or even own up that he was the person that had been reading it. He asked why I was getting so worked up over a newspaper, it was, after all over a week old. I responded that this was the last newspaper that I had been able to buy, we hadn't seen a Spar ship since. I asked him why this was. He shrugged and rolled his eyes. I told him that he had made a mistake, he had taken a left at Venus instead of a right and now we were lost. What kind of a Navigation Officer did he think he was? "How do you even navigate?" was my question to him. He stood for a while pondering my question, then his face lit up and he put his right hand in his pocket and pulled out a compass. He stood looking at the compass for a long while and then said "That is strange! On Earth this compass helped me find my way all the time, but out here in space the needle keeps going around and around, and around..." As he was saying this, his head went around in circles as if he was following the spinning needle. I interrupted him. "Excuse me! Do you use a two-dimensional compass to navigate through three-dimensional space?" He nodded, "yeah, I can't understand why it doesn't work here. By the way, what is two dimensional and three dimensional?" Aha! There was a question that I could answer, or so I thought. I started... "Well two dimensional is... three dimensional is what you can see through those funny glasses you get at the cinema. Anyway, I think that this question is best answered by our Science Officer." I went to the intercom to call out to Shanks, for him to come to the living quarters. I added that there was a matter of urgency, just to get him here. Not long after I had called out to him, did the door open and Shanks came running in, stuttering "Where is the fire?" I reassured him that there was no fire, but we needed him to explain two and three dimensions to us. Shanks looked nervous, then pointed to something behind us and said, "Isn't that a herd of stampeding Wildebeest over there?" Both myself and Hermitage turned to take a look, however we couldn't see any Wildebeest anywhere. After a short while of looking we turned back to Shanks, who seemed to hurriedly put something into his pocket. "Sirs, if you calm down, I will explain two-dimension, three-dimension and also one dimension to you." We calmed down and Shanks pulled out a white board from one of the wardrobes. He then commenced with explaining the different dimensions, and I can't speak for Hermitage, but I can sure tell you that I didn't understand much of what he was saying. When Shanks was finished all I could do was nod and say: "Well that explains that!" and then I left it at that. I suspect Hermitage did too.

"Well with that matter out of the way, it only leaves us with the other matter!" Both Shanks and Hermitage answered in unison: "What matter?" "That matter!" I said, pointing at the newspaper.

Shanks bent over the newspaper and examined it closely. After a while he stood up straight and said "I know what it is Sir! It is a newspaper, it is called The Jupiter Evening Post, additionally it is one week old. There, I have solved the matter for you!" Shanks looked smug. "No! No! No! that is not what the matter is about!" At this point I was so angry that I had difficulties breathing. I grabbed Shanks by his shirt collar and hoisted him up against a wall. There was fear in his eyes. "The matter!" I said between my forced breaths "Is that someone has been reading my newspaper, before I got a chance to read it. Hermitage says it isn't him, so it must be you!" Shanks tried to stutter out a reply, but Hermitage beat him to it. "It was Baz! Yeah, Baz likes to read the newspaper while sitting in his favourite chair, smoking his pipe." I turned my head to look with disbelief at Hermitage. "Who is Baz? There is no Baz on this ship!" Hermitage nodded "Yeah! There is a Baz on this ship, he is the ship's engineer and he is standing right there!" Hermitage pointed to an empty piece of space in the room. I let go of Shanks, who fell, panting for air, to the floor. I turned to face Hermitage. "This ship does not have an Engineer. This ship has never had an engineer. There is no one called Baz on this ship! Do. You. Get. It!" Shanks finally got his breath back and said: "But Sir, Baz is standing right there!" Again, a finger was pointed at an empty piece of space in the room. I waved my arm around in the area where they had been pointing and didn't touch anything. "You guys are crazy! Or you are trying to make me crazy! Right! I will need to punish the both of you. There is no brig onboard and I can't return you to Earth as we are lost..." At this Shanks interrupted me by stuttering "Lost? Did you say we were lost? Just how lost are we?" I did a hand gesture pointing to Hermitage, who showed Shanks his compass. Then Shanks did the oddest of things. He started to dance around singing that we were lost, and hooray we were lost. Odd, very odd. But I would find out the reason for this later on. And you will too later on in my story. Then it might not seem so odd to you. At least it didn't to me. But again, I digress.

I made the both of them clean the whole ship from top to bottom *using only toothbrushes. Shanks seemed to revel in the cleaning duty, but Hermitage kept complaining. I guess punishing Hermitage was enough to make me happy, at least for a while.*

It wasn't until later on that evening that I got a chance to read The J.E.P. and after reading it, I re-read it, again and again, until I felt content with all the articles. I folded up the paper and was just about to place it on the table when I saw the picture on the front page. I had read the article half a dozen times and knew it off by heart, but I hadn't really paid much attention to the picture. Until now… The article on the front page was about the missing heir to the throne of England. He was the heir of Elizabeth II, who was starting to feel her age, she was nigh upon 450 years old, and was just about ready to hand over the throne to her great, great, great, great grandson, or something like that. But the heir had suddenly vanished into thin air. There were theories that he had been kidnapped, or that he had been abducted by aliens. The Uranians were prime suspects, although they hadn't managed to create ships that could traverse the distance from Uranus to Earth. The news wasn't news to me, I had heard about the vanishing heir to the throne before I left to go to Spar fleet command. But it was the picture that intrigued me. I hadn't really paid much attention to the looks of the young prince, but having his picture in front of me had sparked off something in my mind. I reached for a pencil and starting drawing on the picture. When I had finished drawing, the heir of the throne looked familiar. Very familiar! Indeed so familiar that I knew exactly where he was. "Hermitage!" I shouted out.

When Hermitage entered the living quarter, I confronted him with the picture in the newspaper. He tried to deny it at first, but then broke down and cried. After crying for a while, he stopped suddenly, looked up at me and pulled off his wig. When next he spoke, the drawl was gone. "I see there is no point in trying to deny it anymore. What are you going to do? We are lost, and there is no known way of getting me back to Earth." I asked him why he had done it. "Can't you understand the pressure of taking over the throne from… her! She is so demanding, and I'm pretty sure that she would be around even after I took over the throne, continuing to bark orders at me, telling me that I'm a failure, just like my father, and his father, and his father, and his father, and his father before me. Can't you see, my only resort for having a normal life was to run away. I bought the wig and the rags at a second-hand shop, learnt how to speak differently then headed for the nearest space port. I was taken up to Spar Fleet command, hoping to get a job onboard a ship. The first ship I saw was this ship. I liked the name of it and decided to take on the name Hermitage. Soon after I was confronted by General Ifo who drafted me as a Navigation Officer for this ship. Well you know the rest. And if it is all the same to you, I'd prefer to keep up the appearance around Shanks and Baz please. Don't let anyone else know." I nodded and he put his wig back on and seemed to shrink back down to his usual Hermitage size.

The surprises didn't stop there. A few days after that revelation I came across a video that proved to be pretty entertaining. I didn't know what to expect when I started it up. At the beginning of the video there was only an empty park bench, but then a blonde woman came into view. She had a very interesting message. Very interesting indeed. This was her message: "Rupert! You scoundrel! Do you think you can leave your wife and not give me any of your... I mean our money. You better get back to me with the money now Rupert! It is mine! The money is mine! I will hunt you to the ends of the Earth for it! Give it to me now!" and that was the end of the video. I had my suspicions of who Rupert was. I called out for... Shanks... He entered after a few minutes and I showed him the video. He went pale and started to stutter. "I see..." I said. "Care to explain?" Shanks, or Rupert, stuttered incomprehensibly again for a few moments, then cleared his throat, stuttered some more then calmed down a bit. He composed himself and started to tell me his story. "I was never a popular person, not as a child, not as a teenager and not as an adult. My interests were not in sports or going out to the pub getting drunk. My interests were in playing Dungeons and Dragons with my friends. My imaginary friends, as

I didn't have any real ones. Every Friday, since I turned 18, I bought a lottery ticket, and every week I was disappointed that I didn't win anything. That was until that Friday, the thirteenth of March last year. I went to my usual corner-shop and bought my lottery ticket, went home and discovered that I had won the grand slam, the big one, the full ten million pounds. At first, I couldn't believe my eyes. I checked, and double-checked, but no matter how many times I checked and double-checked, it remained the same... I was a millionaire. I cashed in my prize and ended up on the first page of the local newspaper, can you believe it. And can you believe that I suddenly became very popular, I got loads of friends, that wanted to hang out at the pub with me, they even let me buy them all the rounds, just to show how much I meant to them. Then I met Rosie, the oh so beautiful Rosie. The first thing she said to me was that she loved me and had always loved me even when we were at school together. Strange that I don't remember her showing any interest in me back then, she was always hanging out with the popular guys. But I wasn't going to complain. She took me home and taught me things that no Dungeon and Dragons game had ever taught me. It was amazing. The next morning she started talking about her moving in with me and sharing all my stuff with her. I thought it sounded like a good idea and she moved in. She started asking me questions about my winnings, my bank account details, online banking details, etc. It got to a point when I started to have my doubts about her. Was she really in love with me, or was she only after my money? Then the accidents started happening. I say accidents, but I think they were more than accidents. I can't be sure though. I almost got hit by a car, cables and plugs were suddenly giving off extreme amount of electricity, but only on the appliances that I used, never on the appliances that Rosie used. There were other incidents too, things fell out of windows, which luckily missed me. I decided that I would hide the money away and escape my life, away from Rosie. So I did... I hid the money away, then created clues as to the whereabouts, then I went to a memory-wipe clinic to get rid of the memory of where I had hid the money. I remember everything else, but not that particular memory. I then went on the run. It was about that time that that video was sent to my email address. And I guess I should have deleted it from the hard drive after downloading it, but I guess I forgot and now you found it and the secret is all out." I nodded but urged Shanks, Rupert, to continue his story. "The clues are amongst my belongings, but I don't know which things are clues and which are just my belongings. So I have got a lot of money, but I don't know where it is. Anyways... After receiving that message from Rosie, I decided that it would be best to escape Earth all together for some time. I headed to the nearest space port and soon found myself in Spar Fleet Command, standing in a hangar of a new Patrol Ship called Hermitage Shanks. Something in the name appealed to me and I decided that I would take on the name of Shanks and sign up as crew on this ship. Before I could do anything more, I was approached by General Ifo, who asked me to become the Science Officer onboard this ship. I agreed at once, and well, you know the rest. Please don't tell the others!" I promised that I wouldn't.

Life onboard The Hermitage Shanks went on, and we soon found ourselves low on food. We used the long-range scanners to search for habitable planets that might offer up some food. To our surprise we did find a planet and it had food, not just any food, but our favourite food, Swedish Meatballs. The Meatballs were growing on trees all over the planet and we picked the whole planet clean, as we replenished our stock. That was a fun outing. We then had an incident with an errant asteroid that was heading towards us. We didn't have a chance to use any of our weaponry on it or do any evasive actions to avoid it, but instead we placed Hermitage in front of the window, and his stench repelled the errant asteroid. Fun times!

It was after this that things started to get a whole lot stranger. One night I was having trouble sleeping, it felt as if we were travelling backwards or sideways through time or something. I was suddenly aware of someone standing next to my bunk. I looked up at the someone, expecting to see Hermitage or Shanks standing there, but to my surprise it was a complete and utter stranger. I jumped out of my bunk and faced the stranger. "Who are you?" I asked him. "Do you not know? I am the Engineer, I am Baz!" It was unbelievable, I couldn't believe what I was seeing, or hearing. How could it be Baz? He didn't exist! Or did he? Or was I just going crazy? Again I was told that he was Baz, the Engineer. "We haven't got much time." He said. "In order to save the universe, we must act quickly." He then asked me to follow him and we headed to the Bridge. When we reached the Bridge, Hermitage and Shanks were already there. I asked Baz to tell them what he had told me. Both Hermitage and Shanks said in unison "But Baz isn't here!" I told them that he was standing right next to me. I turned to Baz and pointed to him. They still said they couldn't see him. I asked Baz what was going on. "I think it is because we are in the proximity of entering my Universe/ When we were fully in your Universe, you couldn't see me, but they could. Now as we enter my Universe, you can see me, but for some reason they can't. Isn't that just one great mystery!" I didn't know what to say. I asked Baz what we were doing in his Universe. "In order to save your Universe you have to travel through mine and charge this ship with the energies that are native here. Then you will have to return to your Universe and release that energy and win the war, thus saving your Universe." "That Sounds simple enough!" I said and immediately regretted it. "What do you mean by your Universe and our Universe?" "Have you never heard of the Multiverse?" I shook my head. "I'm sure that Shanks will explain if you ask him nicely." I did. Shanks looked nervous, then pointed to an area behind myself and said "Oh, isn't that an obvious distraction over there!" Both myself and Hermitage looked in that direction, trying to see what the distraction was, but failing to do so. We turned around just in time to see Shanks put an object in to his trouser pocket. "Right Sirs, if you calm down, I will tell you about the Multiverse." And boy did he ever. It turns out that there isn't only one Universe. There is in fact an unlimited amount of Universes. Some are pretty similar to ours, and some are as different as they can possibly be. For example, in one Universe it could still be the Dark Ages as America wasn't discovered until early 20th century.

*In another Universe, The Romans discovered the American
continents and set up fortresses all across the lands with a capital
placed where Panama is in our Universe. Just as an explanation to
you Mr Best, we come from different Universes too. In your
Universe there was never a war with the Uranians and that might
not be the only difference. Do you see what I mean?* I did, although
I might have to ask William to explain it all to me later. *We flew
through Baz' Universe all the while we were gathering complex
energy, which was charging our ship. Suddenly Baz shouted out
"Now!" and before I knew what was happening, we passed
through the barrier between his Universe and ours. Straight into a
battle between Spar Fleet and the Uranians. I could no longer see
or hear Baz, so I asked Hermitage and Shanks to act as middle-
men and relay messages between us. Baz ordered me to fly at full
throttle towards Uranus. I did as he bid. As we reached the blue
giant planet, he told me to hit a certain sequence on the panel in
front of me. Again, I did as he bid. By hitting the buttons on the
panel in that sequence I released all the complex energy that we
had gathered in Baz' Universe and it enveloped the entire planet
and suddenly all the Uranian ships stopped working. The war was
over. We had won and I had done it! Me! Flush Jordan! I steered
The Hermitage Shanks back to Spar Fleet and was met with cheers
from everyone there. A messenger came and told me that Colonel
Oon wished to see me at once. Upon entering his office, I saw two
other, unknown to me, gentlemen sitting in the chairs in front of the
Colonel's desk. They got up and introduced themselves as Senator
Bog and Governor John. They continued to explain to me the real
reason why I had been demoted. It hadn't been because I was so
popular, it was because I was the only person that could have
pulled off what I just pulled off. They knew that I would never have
agreed to remove myself from the heat of the battle voluntarily, so
they arranged for my demotion to Captain of a Patrol Ship. The
Patrol Ship, was an experimental ship that had been constructed
with a Multiverse drive, which allowed it to jump between the
different Universes. In order to get the right crew, certain other
events were put into motion which led to the heir to the throne of*

England, deciding to escape and don the disguise of Hermitage and thus become the Navigation officer onboard the Hermitage Shanks. A rigged lottery ticket led to a gamer becoming incredibly popular over-night and thus leading him to escaping Earth and becoming the Science Officer onboard the Hermitage Shanks. The only person that was aware of the full plan from the beginning was Baz, who was from a parallel Universe. Baz had agreed to carry out the plan of getting the ship lost in space for the reason of bonding the crew together and preparing them for what was to come. It was a lot to take in, but when they offered me a medal for my deed, I turned them down and returned to the ship. I had made my mind up, I would traverse the multiverse and see how things had turned out there. So, there you have it, that is how we ended up here, the patrol ship is now working as a Merchant ship. At some point we will leave this Universe and move into another, but for the time being we will remain here and help you it seems. Flush smiled. It had been one heck of a story. Hard to believe it all, but the way he told it, it almost most certainly had to have be all true, no matter how odd it seemed.

An alarm suddenly started up. *"We are approaching a checkpoint of the protective shield that separates The Inner Circle from the rest of the Universe. I will send them my licence code."* Flush keyed in a long sequence of numbers and letters into the console in front of him then hit enter. It seemed to take an eternity before there was a response. *"This is checkpoint ZA45, we have received your licence code and can confirm that it is legit. We will be opening the grid at the attached coordinates, please ensure that you are safe inside within the allocated time or the grid will be powered up again. I can assure you that you do not want to be in the wrong place when the grid powers up. Over!"* Flush checked the attached coordinates and steered the ship towards them. As we came closer, I could see the power grid. It stretched in all directions and there were nodes that kept the grid power running and ensured that specific sections of the grid could be powered down to allow ships to fly through. It seemed like a good defensive system to keep unwanted people out, or even keep people in. As

we flew through the section of the grid that was powered down, I caught a glimpse of a small space station close by. I pointed to it. *"That is checkpoint ZA45, the guys that hailed us. There are thousands of these checkpoints located all along this grid. They decide who gets to come in and who gets to come out."*
We passed by them and Flush set us on course with the only inhabited planet within The Inner Circle. The planet where I had come from. The planet where I would, probably, meet my father. For better or for worse.

Chapter 18

The planet was gigantic. I guess it was far larger than my brother's planet. We were escorted into land in a docking bay, close to the Merchant quarters. That made sense as we were, after all, in a Merchant ship. Flush got the ship set down without incident. As we opened our doors, we were met by a welcoming committee consisting of the head of the Merchant guild and Docking bay Master. The Docking bay Master needed to be paid for Flush to keep his ship docked there. The head of the Merchant guild needed to ensure that Flush had a sufficient trading licence. Flush produced credits for The Docking bay Master and his Trading licence to the head of the Merchant guild. When they were content, they silently nodded to Flush and left. Flush told me: *"The Royal Palace is in that direction!"* He pointed in the direction slightly to the rear of the docking bay. *"If you need to leave, we will be here for about a week, then we will be on our way. A week is as long as I'm licenced to be here to trade wares. Good luck James! Hope you find your father, and everything turns out alright for you!"* I thanked him and his crew and left with William to find our way to the Royal Palace.

It was going to prove more difficult to find our way to the palace than I would have thought. The streets were a maze and were cluttered with people, stalls and animals. This was the Merchant quarter. How far away was the palace? It was difficult to tell. I could see the spires looming high up over the roof tops in the far distance, but it was difficult to gauge the distance. We stopped at a stall and asked one of the merchants if he knew how we could get to the palace. He told us that he wasn't aware of the way there, as he had never been, but he suggested that we go to the nearest tavern and ask the landlord, and if he didn't know, then he might know someone who did. It was a long-shot, but worth it if we could find our way. The merchant pointed out a tavern that was located a bit of the way further down the street. We pushed our way through the crowd of people and animals and entered the tavern, called The Smokey Pear. Inside The Smokey Pear it was just about as crowded as it was outside. We pushed our way to the bar and tried to get the attention of the landlord. He was a fat man with thick curly hair, wearing a greasy apron. I guess tavern landlords look almost the same across the entire Universe. We finally caught his attention and he walked on over to us. *"What can I get you gents?"* we ordered the local version of beer and then asked him how we could find our way to the Royal Palace. The landlord grimaced and asked why we would ever want to go there. I didn't tell him the real reason, just that I had a personal message for the King. *"Nothing good will come out of you going there. The King has been a recluse for as long as anyone can remember. The gossip goes that he lost all his sons and hasn't been outside the Palace since then. There used to be banquets and balls at the Palace all the time, but now... nothing! No one has seen the King in ages, and he used to travel around the streets of the capital all the time. But that was then, now he never leaves the Palace, there are no banquets or balls. Just rumours of a very miserable and lonely King. Anyway if you do need to get there, head north to the Guild quarter, then on to the Crafters terrace, once you have made your way through the Crafters terrace head on to Temple Square and beyond that is the Palace Gardens, people are allowed to wander around the gardens, however no one is allowed to approach the Royal Palace, on pain of death. Best of luck now."* We thanked the Landlord and left the Tavern. After looking around, we managed to find a sign that showed the direction to the Guild quarter. Once we left the Merchant quarter behind and reached the Guild quarter there were fewer people and animals around. There were also no stalls. The streets were lined with buildings with signs outside stating what kind of Guild was inside. There was the Merchant guild, the Artists guild, the Smiths guild, the Armorers guild, the Assassins guild, and many more. It was interesting to read all the signs and realise that it reminded me of how things had been in Europe during the Medieval times. Pretty fascinating. After a while we came upon the sign showing the direction to the Crafters terrace. We headed there and found workshops that crafted items like weapons, armour, jewellery, clothes, shoes, barrels, and much more. Again, I was reminded of Medieval times back in Europe. As we walked down the streets, we looked into the workshops and observed as the different crafters made their wares. Wares that would later be sold in the Merchant quarter. Very reminiscent of Medieval times in Europe. How often could I think and say that? Not enough apparently. Everything I saw, everywhere I looked, I was reminded of how things had looked in Europe during the early to mid-medieval period. The buildings, the workshops, the signs on the workshops, taverns and shops, the way people dressed, just about everything was in the way that I remembered it from my time in that period. It was an odd experience to be on another planet and be in the midst of this… this… for me historical period experience… thingy… I didn't really want to rush on towards the Royal Palace, instead I wanted to savour my surroundings as much as possible. But soon enough we crossed over a bridge which took us to the Temple Square. It would be interesting to see what type of deity or deities that they worshiped here. In the middle of the square there was a huge building which I assumed was the Temple. It reminded me of a mix of Romano-Greco Gothic style and some other styles that I didn't know the names of, almost as if it had started off as one type of building and then someone had built on to it with a different type of style, and then another and another, until it was this huge building which must serve as the place of worship for the entire City, it was surely huge enough for everyone to get a seat in it. Although I was sure that my guess was correct, I wanted to find out for myself. I told William that I wanted to go inside and have a look around. William objected, saying that we should make our way to the Royal Palace to meet my father. I replied that I really did want to meet my father, however this Temple was far too interesting to be given a miss.

We walked up to the gigantic wooden doors and pushed them open. They opened with far too much of a creaky noise, which echoed throughout the huge hall. Inside the Temple, it wasn't all too different than inside any given Catholic church back on Earth. There were rows upon rows of benches for the people to sit in. There were statues and frescoes lining the walls, there were thousands upon thousands of lit candles all over the place. I studied the statues and the frescoes and there seemed to be a story being told of some sort. In fact, it looked a lot like the story that my brother had told me, after studying it more intently I came to the realisation that it was in fact the story of me, my brothers, my father and the attempts on my life. But looking at the paintings, it appeared to be my brothers that were behind the assassination attempts on my life. I needed to go find my father and find out the truth, once and for all. But first, I wanted to finish my visit inside this amazingly huge Temple. At the far end of the Temple, in what would be the front of it, there was a huge statue of a man. I went up and looked at it. The features of the man looked familiar, I just couldn't put my finger on why he looked familiar, until William said that he thought the man looked like me. *It could be a statue of your father? It would make sense that he is the deity that they worship here, if he is the ruler of this planet and the whole Inner Circle, then it would make sense. Don't you think?"* I didn't know what to think. But after what William just said, it did make sense that the statue was a likeness of my father. But did the people worship him like a God? Wouldn't that be bizarre? Surely, he was just their King and that is why there is a statue of him here. They do things differently here than on Earth, that must be it. They don't worship Gods here, just revere their Royalty. That is why my story was painted upon the walls. I was part of the Royal mythos. How long ago did it happen? I had ended up on Earth during the time of the Dinosaurs, that was at least 65 million years ago. That is a long time to have been away from home. Were all people here immortals too? Or were we only a specific breed amongst mortals? I should have asked my brother more about it when I was there, but I really didn't think about it then. These paintings have raised a whole load of new questions which I hope will be answered. Did I really want them answered though? Would the answers give birth to more questions? Where would it all end? I told William that it was time for us to move on. Time to go and meet my father and find out exactly what had happened and hopefully get my lost memories back.

Chapter 19

We left the Temple and headed towards the Palace Gardens. Luckily the Gardens were open to the public to be able to wander around in, which meant that we could get all the way up to the gates of the Palace with no problems. Outside the Gates stood two guards. They were armed with spears and had swords attached to their belts. Their uniforms were a darkish blue colour and their hats were tall and had, what looked like, a peacock feather attached to a band that surrounded it. Their boots were of leather and knee-high and looked as if they had been meticulously polished. The looks on the guards faces were stern and unmoving. We went up to them and were stopped by the guards crossing their spears to stop us from approaching the gate. Their faces were still stern and unmoving, even as they spoke. *Halt! No one may enter through these gates! By order of His Royal Majesty, King Arton, first of his name, ruler of Aesgaard, descendant of Non, the all-seer, Saviour of the people and righter of wrongs."* That was a lot to take in all at once. I cleared my throat and said: *And I am Avalon, first of my name, son of Arton, first of his name, also known as James Best, also known as The Blackpanther, Winner of battles and traveller of the stars.* At the mention that I was the son of the King, the faces of both "guards dropped ever so slightly. *How can you be son of Arton? What did you say your name was?* I repeated the first part again, just telling them that my name was Avalon. The guards looked uneasy at each other, then at me. They whispered intensely with each other for a few moments, then looked at me. *This is impossible, Prince Avalon died a long time ago. You can't be him. I stress this point again: You can not be him!"* And yet I was. *Allow me to go and meet my father, I'm sure he will be happy to see me. However if he finds out that his son returned after all this time away and was stopped from coming home by the two of you, can you imagine what he would do to you."* The unmoving faces, were no longer unmoving. They suddenly went grey and looked incredibly worried. It looked like they could imagine what would happen to them. One of the guards told me that he would go up to the palace and get someone that might be able to verify if I was who I claimed to be. He saluted me and then turned to salute his comrade before heading up to the Palace.

It took a while before I could see the guard returning from the Palace with someone tagging along. As they came closer I could see that the man that was with the guard, was a short, round man, with hardly any hair on his head, but what he lacked on top he made up for on his chin. He had a large bushy beard, made up of mainly brown hair, but there were grey and white specks here and there. His face was red, as if he wasn't used to move as fast as the guard was making him. They soon reached us and the short man came up to me. He scrutinised me closely. After a short time of checking me from top to toe his face shone up. *Well I'll be... I never thought that I would ever lay eyes on you again my Prince.* He turned to the guards. *This is Prince Avalon. I will take him, and his friend, to see his father now.* The guards looked slightly worried. The short man noticed this and told them not to worry about any repercussions, they had done their job well. They couldn't be faulted for not recognising their prince, as they hadn't been born at the time when I had been living here. The guards looked relieved and returned to their duty of guarding the gate with their unmoving faces. The short man, who introduced himself as Minister Njord, led us up to the Royal Palace. When we reached the huge doors, he took out a huge metal key and unlocked the equally huge metal lock, then he pulled the doors until they swung open, silently. If the doors to the Temple had been incredibly loud in their opening, these doors were incredibly silent, there wasn't any noise that would alert anyone to the fact that the doors were in fact opening. Njord urged us on through the open doors and along a corridor, which was edged with tall pillars. The corridor was badly lit, however every so often there was a burning torch attached to a pillar, which gave off a bit of light to its vicinity. We walked on for ages and the corridor seemed to go on forever.

Finally we came to another set of huge doors, which weren't locked, so Njord pushed them open and we walked on through. On the other side of the doors there was a huge room. A huge room which seemed to be empty, no noise, no people, no statues, no anything. But wait… I was wrong… Up ahead in the far end of the room I could just about make out something, but I couldn't for the life of me see exactly what it was from the distance. Njord urged us on and as we approached the object at the far end of the room it was suddenly made clear that it was a throne, and on the throne, sat a man. I say sat, but it was more like slumped. The man was slumped on the throne. As we got even closer, it was clear that the man slumped on the throne was a very sad man, perhaps the crown was heavy on his head, perhaps he was sad over the loss of his sons, perhaps it was something else. Njord suddenly made a gesture with his hands to stop us. We did as he bid. Njord then approached the throne and addressed the King.

Your Majesty, King Arton, First of your name. He bowed. The King seemed indifferent. *I have brought you your missing son.* The King didn't react. He still seemed totally indifferent to anything that was being said to him, or perhaps he didn't register that anyone else was there. *Your son! Your son, Avalon! He is here! He has returned! Please Your Majesty! Gaze upon your son! He has returned! It is time to rejoice!"* At these words the King turned his gaze upon us and it was clear that he wasn't truly looking at any of us. After a while though, his facial expression suddenly started to change. It was as if something within him was stirring with recognition. He looked at me. No, it was almost as if he was looking through me. Through my very soul. Life seemed to return to his eyes and his face, slowly but surely. His head tilted slightly to the left as he looked at me again. *Can it be?* He said with a low and croaky voice. He sat up straight on his throne, looked at me again from that new angle. Then got up from his throne. It wasn't a quick or easy manoeuvre, as it looked like he hadn't moved from the throne in a very long time. Joints creaked and popped as he got up. He then walked over to me on unsteady legs, looked me over again then fell to his knees, crying. Through his tears and sobbing he kept repeating the same words over and over again: *"My son, my son, you have returned to me!"* I too fell to my knees and embraced him, then helped him up to his feet. He looked at me, still with disbelief in his eyes. *How can this be? I thought you dead for sure. Yet here you are, in front of me, alive and well.* He took a step back from me to be able to get a better look at me. *Come sit with me and tell me how it is that you have returned to me.* I sat down next to him and started telling him my story as much as I could tell him, as much as I knew. I didn't tell him of the story version that Avatar had told me. I wanted him to tell me his version without any bias from that version of the story. I asked him if he could tell me the sequence of events that had led to my exile from my home. He looked sad at having to have to remember these events. He cleared his throat.

Where to start? I guess at the moment, starting from the beginning is as good as anywhere. But what is the beginning? It was so long ago, that my memories might be slightly muddled, but I do think I can remember most of it as it happened.

A very long time ago, on the planet of Aeden, which lies inside the Inner Core, which you can see if you go outside and look in to the sky. The Inner Core is the absolute centre of the universe and within the core there is only one planet. The planet of Aeden, that is where you were born, and where I was too. Please have patience with me as I tell you this story as it is both long and eventful. There is a lot of things that happened that you will need to remember for the future.

In the beginning, when the Universe was created by Non, he created one planet that would act as a template for every other planet throughout the entire Universe. This was the planet Aeden. He created me in his image, I never figured out if that meant that I looked like him, or if it was only his traits that were copied unto me. I still have never met Non myself, so it is difficult to know. I found myself wandering around Aeden and loving the life that Non had created to keep me company and well-fed. Non then offered me a companion. Someone who looked like me, but not exactly like me. A female version of myself. She was beautiful and we fell in love.

The lovely Endra and I were inseparable as we made Aeden our home. Everything was paradise for us, but we were the only two of our species. We asked Non to provide us with some more of our own species that we could interact with. Non answered us and provided us with a huge amount of men and women of our species to interact with. We quickly became the power elite on Aeden and started to construct a city to live in. In the midst of the city we had a palace built. I ruled as King and Endra ruled as my Queen. More and more of us were born and the city was soon overpopulated. Amongst this boom in population you were born. The King and Queen had given birth to an heir to the throne. That was great news for everyone. Well perhaps not for everyone, but I'll get to that part in a bit.

Paradise City was soon to become something entirely different, Endra discovered that not only did we not age like the animals did, but we had powers over mind and matter. Endra discovered that she was able to, not only, read minds, but also manipulate minds to do what she wanted the people to do. I had that ability too, still do I guess. But I disagreed with Endra, I didn't think we should be using that power. Manipulating and controlling others wasn't ethical. Endra thought it was a good way of getting people to do what she wanted them to do, to love her and obey her. This caused a schism between us, but not only between us, sides were taken and soon a civil war broke out. My beloved Endra and I were on opposing sides. I knew that it wouldn't come to a good ending. My main concern was you. I wanted to make sure that you were safe. I managed to get you out from the Palace and from Paradise City and safely tucked away in our base in the mountains. We waged war on your mother and her supporters. Not really sure if they supported her of their own free will or if they were being controlled. We had one sure way of avoiding mind control, by enveloping our heads in hats that were lined with lead. For some reason Endra's mind controlling powers couldn't break through lead. Perhaps because that metal is so porous, perhaps there is another reason. At least it worked. Anyone wearing a hat which was lead-lined couldn't have their mind read or controlled. This *was of course very helpful when we attacked Paradise City. Endra didn't know that we were coming and wasn't prepared. But that still didn't help us. Her army of supporters was greater than ours. There is something you need to know on how your mother wages war. She is very adept in what she calls "Mind Games", I call it "Mind wars" it isn't pretty and I hate having to do it. I hate doing it! In short it means that you enter the mind of your opponent, or they enter yours and within the mind a battleground is set up. The opponents then battle it out within the mind. What causes problems is when the opponent that is within the other opponent's mind decides to pull the battle in to their mind. Then the other opponent can do the same thing, and the other, and the other, until everyone is confused as to which mind they are in. Doing this also has it's dangers, for each time you get pulled in to the other mind, you go down one level. In order to get out of the mind war you will need to get out through all the layers. I've seen friends succumb to the mind war, they were pulled down so deep by trickery, thinking that they would be able to win the mind war in the battlefield of their own mind. This is a mistake, if you are up against someone as adept at Mind wars like your mother, there can be no easy victory. Lifeless husks with no minds left in their body. That was all that was left of them! Let me tell you again, my son, there can be no easy victory against your mother. We were utterly defeated and had to retreat back to our base. It seemed utterly hopeless. A decision was made. I was too important to the cause to risk losing, and in extension so were you. A space ship was built that would take the both of us and a few other loyal supporters through what we called the Mesh, to whatever was on the other side. The Mesh was nothing other than what we now know as the border to the Inner Core. It is indeed aptly named. It is a mesh of conflicting forces, that can easily destroy any ship that travels through it. That is unless you are in possession of a ship that has been specifically made to withstand conflicting forces. It would have to be able to absorb and recycle kinetic energy instantaneous. Of course, not one of us had any knowledge how to build a ship that could traverse the Mesh. Indeed, we hadn't ever created any space faring crafts. There had been no need as our planet was the only one in our part of the Universe. Back then we of course didn't have concepts of other planets. All we knew was that we lived on a world that we called home. Anything beyond was unknown and inconceivable. But with desperate times come desperate ideas. The scientists amongst us, started to conceive the idea that there might be more worlds. With those ideas, came the inventions that allowed them to discover the Mesh. They created probes to send up in to space to find out what the Mesh was. What they found out scared us all, almost worse than going to battle with your mother again. Our scientists used the data that they gathered from the probes and managed to construct a space faring craft that should be able to make its way through the Mesh in one piece. It was a huge gamble, but we needed to do something. On the day that the ship was completed, I got on the ship, together with you and a few other selected supporters. The ship was launched from our hidden base in the mountains and within a few minutes we had left our world behind and were heading towards the scariest and most dangerous journey of our life. When the ship hit the Mesh it felt as if we had been hit by something huge, like for example a large boulder, then it felt as if something was trying to pull us apart. The forces within the Mesh was doing its best to destroy us, but we were lucky. We were lucky! I don't think we knew at the time just how lucky we were. I can't tell you how long we spent within the Mesh, it felt like an eternity, and it felt like no time at all. It's difficult to explain, it was if time itself didn't exist within the Mesh. All I know is the sigh of relief we all released when we finally emerged on the other side. We stopped the ship and took a well needed rest before continuing our journey.*

Once we had rested, we started to look around in the area in which we had arrived in. After looking for a long while we came across a planet in the distance. We steered our ship towards it, hoping that it would become our new home. Back then we didn't have the concept that not all planets can support life. Luckily though this one did, and we made it our new home. No other planets in the vicinity were able to support life, that is why we have never inhabited any other planet within the Inner Circle. But that is alright, we are all content being here. Well, perhaps not everyone. You see, after we made this planet our new home, we built up this city and this palace and everything that you can see. You were my only child and I felt that you missed your friends from our old home. That is when I decided to create you a couple of brothers. I asked the scientists if it was possible to create copies of you. They went away to ponder upon the request. They finally returned to me with a solution, they called it cloning. They would take a bit of my genetic material and clone it. I asked them to clone two brothers for you. Your brothers were grown in a lab and were given false memories of their childhood, making them think that they too had come from the old world. When they were fully grown they were released from the lab and welcomed in to our home. You welcomed your brothers with open arms and you three became inseparable. You would do everything together. You each had your favourite Sleipner that you would take out for long rides to the beautiful wilderness. You particularly loved the Mill falls. You would all spend hours there, sitting, dangling your feet over the edge of the falls and talking about things that young men talk about, girls and parties. It was a true golden age for all of us. But then something happened. It was made clear that one of my supporters that had come along with me from the old world was a traitor, an agent of your mother. He or she was sowing seeds of discord amongst everyone else. Factions were created and sides were taken. You became the prime target. What I didn't realise at the time, and if I had then things would have developed in a completely different way, was that your brothers had become part of the faction that supported your mother. They became the main agents involved in your assassination attempts, due to their proximity and access to you. I lost count of all the attempts on your life. Then came the fateful day when I thought they had succeeded. You had been out riding on your favourite Sleipner when all of a sudden an arrow hit your head and pierced your skull. When you were finally found and taken back to the palace, it was made clear that the arrow head was made of the only metal that can cause damage to our kind. The

144

metal is only available from the old world, so it had to have been supplied by someone that had connections to the old world, unless of course the metal had been brought with us when we fled the old world. It was irrelevant where the metal had come from. My main concern was your welfare, and then finding out who had tried to kill you. I had my suspicions that it was one, or both of your brothers, but it was difficult to prove. I got my loyalists to hunt for the culprit or culprits, whilst I stayed by your side, day and night, watching over you. Protecting you from any further attacks. I lost count of all the days and nights that I sat beside you, but one day one of my messengers entered your room and told me that the faction that supported the Queen from the old world had started a full scale revolt in the lower sections of the city. I had to lead my troops in to the battle, with the hope of squashing the rebellion before it got out of hand. What I didn't know, was that the revolt was just a ruse. While I was leading my troops, your brothers snuck in to your room and stole you away. Boris took you on to a space faring ship and made his escape, while Avatar led his troops against mine. When I heard of what had happened I sent three of my fastest space faring ships with the best pilots to make chase and retrieve you. They never returned. When you never returned, I thought you dead. I was saddened, and then angered by your brothers' actions. I declared all out war on your remaining brother and his faction. Most of the traitors were found and put in jail, but Avatar escaped. My intelligence officers informed me that he had set up base on a planet not all too far away, and it would be wise of me to create some kind of defence against him returning with a large army. That is how the concept of the shield was born. The shield is designed to keep unwanted people out of here. Although I soon realised that we couldn't be self-sufficient. Licences were granted to specific merchants that could travel through the shield, as long as their licence was valid. The shield has kept us safe here. We do, however, have a large fleet of space faring ships that we could use any time that we needed to attack Avatar. Now that you are back, my son, perhaps we should do just that. Time to take revenge on him for what he did to you, to us. You

*shake your head? Oh well, never mind, whatever you want my son.
I shall arrange for a banquet to honour your return. These halls
have been too silent for far too long. Ever since you were taken I
drew back in to myself and became a reluctant recluse. But now!
But now, you are back! Let us rejoice! My son has returned!*
And there you have it. My father's side of the story. Different, but
not completely different from the one that my brother told me.
There had been no mention of any prophecy either. And this story
coincided with the pictures that I had seen in the Temple. But did
that make it true? How could I be sure? I had hoped that coming
back home would return my memories to me. Nothing had
happened. Nothing in the slightest. No memories had come
flooding back to me. Wasn't that how it was supposed to work?
Wasn't that how it worked in all those films where people suffered
from amnesia, they came home and suddenly their memories
returned and it all ended with a happily ever after for everyone.
But this isn't a film, this is my life, and my memories aren't
returning just because I returned home. There won't be a happily
ever after ending for me. That metal that the arrowhead had been
made out of must have done irreversible damage to the part of my
mind where memories are kept. And now my father is planning a
banquet in my honour. What next?

Chapter 20

I don't know how my father pulled it off in such a short time. When the evening arrived, we found ourselves in the huge banquet hall, eating and drinking merrily. William commented on the good quality of the wine. I felt like a fish out of water. This was supposed to be my home, where I grew up, I should probably know most of the people present, but couldn't for the life of me remember anyone of them. It put me in a bit of a sombre mood, despite the ambient and light mood of the party. I listened to a group of strangers talking about how great it was to finally have the King open up his Palace for great parties again, and of course it was great to have the Prince back again too. But to me it sounded as if my return was only secondary in importance to them. What did that mean? Had they known me? Was there anyone present in this room that had known me properly and had perhaps called me friend? I sat alone at a table, drinking wine and brooding over the entire bizarre situation. William was off mingling with just about everyone present and my father was busy talking with some important looking men and women.

Suddenly a beautiful woman sat down next to me. *I never thought I would see you again, my love.* I was taken aback. Who was this woman? She was beautiful, no mistake, but did she really know me, or was she just taking a chance? *You look as if you don't remember me.* I shook my head and told her that my memories from my time here were gone. She sighed and looked genuinely saddened by my remark. *I guess your feelings for me are gone too?* I tried very hard to search for any kind of memory or feeling I might have had for this beautiful woman at some point, if I had, I couldn't recall any, however, looking at her I could understand that I would have had feelings for her at some point. I shook my head slowly. *I guess your wound did more damage than we initially thought.* She brushed away my hair to reveal my scar from the arrow wound and touched it, almost reverently. *I can still remember when they brought your lifeless body back to the Palace. I thought you were dead. I cried for what felt like ages. When it was clear that you were still alive, but would most likely never wake up from the lifeless sleep, I cried for weeks. Then your brothers got you away from the Palace and out of my life forever. Or so I thought. When my father told me that you had returned my heart skipped a beat. I have waited for you forever. Never taken another boyfriend or lover. You have been forever in my thoughts and heart.* I didn't know what to say. Except… except… this woman might know the true story of what had happened. Perhaps… just perhaps… the chance was slim that she knew the whole truth, but I needed to know. I told her that I had lost all my memory and had awakened on a distant planet, on which I had lived for untold millennia. I didn't tell her the name or the location of Earth. I'm not sure why I didn't, I just felt that some things should be kept under wraps until I knew exactly who I could trust. I asked her, her name.

You can't even remember my name? She broke down and cried. I put my arm around her shoulder and tried to console her. After a long sobbing bout, she calmed down. At least enough to be able to continue talking. *I'm Brynhilde, we were betrothed. We would have been wed had not the awful thing happened.* I asked her if she knew exactly what had happened. Again she looked saddened. *I remember it as clearly as if it only happened yesterday. You loved to go riding. It was something that we both loved doing. I would have been with you that day, except I had an appointment with the Bridal Boutique to try on wedding dresses. Perhaps things would have turned out differently if I had been with you. Perhaps not. It is something that I have been mulling over all these many years. Anyway, I was at the Bridal Boutique when my hand-maiden came running in with the news that you had been mortally wounded by an arrow to your head and may even be dead. I rushed out of the shop and headed over to the Palace as fast as I could. Your father and brothers were in your room with you. You looked all pale and lifeless in your bed. I leaned over you and kissed your lips. They were so cold. It wasn't the usual warm kiss, like we used to share when we were out on our dates. When I felt your cold lips, that is when I broke down and started my endless crying. I was led away from your room and back to my domicile. My parents tried to console me, but it was to no avail. I knew that you were lost to me. A kiss that cold could only mean one thing. You were already dead. If not completely, then you would be soon. There was nothing left for me. My love was dead. What did I have left to live for? I did contemplate ending my life on several occasions, but my parents stood by me through all the hard times and supported me when I needed them the most. When you were taken away by your brother, Boris, my father told me that it was because they realised that I was still alive and they needed me for something or other. He wouldn't tell me anything else, and I didn't really push for any more information. All I cared about was the chance that you were alive somewhere in the vastness of the Universe. That thought gave me the hope to carry on. That hope has paid off! You have returned to me!* With that she leaned close to me and gave me a warm kiss on my lips. I was taken aback, but let the kiss happen. It felt so good. I responded to her kiss. When our lips finally parted the look on her face was filled with elation and love. She asked me for a dance. Without hesitation I got up and soon found myself on the dancefloor, holding Brynhilde in my arms, spinning around to the slow and melodious music. During our dance we kissed again. A kiss that lasted through at least three dances. Brynhilde had told me her story, but it hadn't given me any answers to the questions that I had about whether it was my father or my brother who was telling the truth. I just wished that my memories would return. That would solve a lot of my dilemma.

My father came over to me and Brynhilde, where we were still standing, embracing each other. He had another man with him. Brynhilde whispered that the other man was her father. I almost let go of her by pure reflex and embarrassment, but still we clung to each other. *I see you two have reunited.* Brynhilde's father said with a smile. *The wedding can now happen as we planned. Albeit a bit delayed.* My father laughed out loud. *Yes, but remember dear*

Brokk, Avalon also has Princely duties to carry out. Brokk looked slightly worried, or perhaps nervous at this remark. *Ah, yes of course my liege, but I hope that won't come in the way of the wedding.* My father shook his head. *No, of course not. It might have to wait a while though, until my son has settled back in. I trust that is ok with you!* That had been no question as far as I could tell. What was going on? Something didn't seem kosher. But one look from Brynhilde made me forget all about the exchange of words between my father and Brokk. *Another dance my love?* How could I refuse? We spun out on to the dance floor again, oblivious to our surroundings. I couldn't remember Brynhilde, but if my feelings for her back then were anything like the feelings I had developed for her in this very short span of time, then I could only say that we had been very much in love. Not only was she beautiful, she also had a very warm and loving personality.

The dance finished and we parted reluctantly from each other's embrace. We stood looking in to each other's eyes for a long time before I asked if I could escort her home. She nodded. We walked from the Palace, through the gardens and out through the outer gates. We walked down the streets to her domicile, which she shared with her parents. It would most likely have been called a mansion on Earth. It was pretty large and had a beautiful garden out front. Even in the darkness, it's beauty was easy to see. We kissed good night and I left her to go in through her door and away from me. I returned to the Palace, feeling giddy as a teenager. Or at least that is what I thought a teenager in love would feel. I had no memories of being a teenager, in love or otherwise.

I got to the Palace and the guards escorted me to my chamber. I fell in to bed and went to sleep almost as soon as my head hit the pillow.

The next morning I awoke and was met by servants that bathed me and clothed me in new clothes. I made sure that my sword was hung on the belt of my new trousers. I would not want to leave that anywhere.

I was then led downstairs to the breakfast room. My father and William were already sitting at the table, having breakfast and seemingly telling jokes. They both looked up at me when I entered the room. *Ah, my son, you have finally surfaced. I daresay you had a most enjoyable evening neh? And a reunion with the lovely Brynhilde, not bad, not bad at all. A wedding between the two of you will strengthen our status. Although I am pretty sure that the two of you are so much in love that anything like the strengthening of houses is only a secondary reason for the wedding.* He laughed again. William smiled at me, with a nod and a wink. I quickly gave him a look that would put out any thoughts like I'm sure he had about what happened between myself and Brynhilde after we left the party. William frowned and then left it at that.

I sat down at the table and the servants brought me my breakfast. I ate heartily of the small feast set out before me.

After I had finished eating, my father addressed William *Well we won't be needing your services any more Mr White. I will arrange for an escort to take you back to the Hermitage Shanks for the passage away from here.* I started protesting, but my father stopped me. *It is alright my son, you are back home now. Your friend doesn't belong here. Strangers are allowed to stay for short times only. I don't allow for strangers to settle here. It is a policy that I put in place to keep my people safe and secure. Your friend may come and visit from time to time, but for living here, you will have to make it without him. You are also getting married to Brynhilde soon, that will mark a huge change in your life. But before you get married you have to take on the governorship over your birth-right.* I must have looked confused to my father as he continued to explain. *Your birth-right is a small planetoid not far away from here. There you will prove to me that you have it in you to rule over the population. If you prove you are more than a capable ruler, you will return here, marry Brynhilde. I will then abdicate the crown in your favour and you will be the King. Sound ok to you?* He didn't really wait for me to answer. *Good! It is settled. Say your farewell to William and get ready for your short trip to your planetoid.* I didn't know what to say. I guess William made it easy, he got up from the table, looked at me, stretched out his hand to me. I got up, took his hand and shook it, then we had a quick embrace and said our good-byes. William then turned away and walked out of the breakfast room, back to the Hermitage Shanks and back to whatever waited for him on the outside of the Inner Circle. I had to accept that I was home now. That I would have to prove myself a good ruler to my father in order for me to get to marry Brynhilde and become the King of Aesgaard.

You have been dressed in your royal garb this morning and are now ready to travel to The Cliff, where you will prove yourself as a ruler over the small population. My father led me out through the door away from the Breakfast room and out of the Royal Palace. We were accompanied by two guards who walked silently behind us. My father led me through the gardens until we reached an area which he told me was the Royal ship yard. He led me to the ship that would take me to The Cliff. I got onboard, but before I did, my father embraced me. *Make me proud son!* The ship's door closed behind me. I was led to a comfortable seat and got strapped in by the stewardess. The pilot called out over the loudspeaker system that we would be taking off in a few minutes, for me to relax and enjoy the short trip. I did as I had been told. I sat back in my chair, drank the drink that the Stewardess offered me. Soon the ship swooped up in to the air and we were on our way.

The pilot had been right, the trip wasn't very long at all. Very soon we landed on the small planetoid, The Cliff, and I was let out of the ship. I had expected some kind of welcoming party, but no one came to meet and greet me as I disembarked the ship.

The ship's door closed and soon the ship swooped almost silently back in to the air again, on its return to Aesgaard. I looked around and saw a small building off in the distance. I headed in that direction.

For a small planetoid, it still seemed pretty big. It took me a pretty long time to reach the building. When I approached it, a group of people exited it and waved their arms at me, shouting *Go back! Don't come here! Go back to Aesgaard!* I was confused. Weren't these people my subjects? Wasn't I supposed to rule here. The group of people reached me and the looks on their faces changed as they saw who I was. One of the men came up to me. *My Prince!*

I didn't see it was you at first. Why are you here? Where have you been? I gave him a brief summary of what had happened to me after I had been taken away by Boris. I then told him why I had come here. All the men in the group sighed heavily and shook their heads. The man that had approached me closed his eyes, sighed again then opened his eyes again, looked intently at me and said something that froze me to my very soul. *You have been duped my Prince. Your father wants you dead. He was behind your assassination attempt. Your brothers did their best to rescue you. We staged an attack to draw your father out from your room, so your brother, Boris, could rescue you. Once your father had figured out what had happened, he retaliated. He sent out his loyalist troops who all but cleansed out all resistance. All that weren't killed off were sent here, to this doomed prison planetoid.* I asked what he meant by doomed. Once again he sighed heavily. *Look over there!* He said, pointing up in to the sky. *Tell me what you see!* I looked in the direction of where he was pointing, but all I could see was what my father had called The Mesh. I told the man that I wasn't sure what I should be seeing. *That!* He said whilst vividly casting his arm in the direction of the sky. *That there is The Mesh! This planetoid is not only our prison, it is also our doom. There are missiles aimed at us that will make this planetoid leave the orbit that it currently holds. Once we leave this safe orbit, we will head slowly, but surely towards The Mesh. I'm sure you know what will happen to us once we enter that hell!* I sure did. After hearing my father's story about his trip through The Mesh I had no desire to travel through it, at least not on a planetoid that would most certainly be pulled to pieces. *Your father will finally get his wish. With your arrival here, he will most assuredly have those missiles fired at us. We will all die in there. He will get rid of you. The prophecy will fail. He will also get rid of the last remnants of the resistance that exist within The Inner Circle. There are no more of the resistance left on Aesgaard. There are only loyalists left there.* I asked if the resistance had been in support of my mother. The man shook his head. *The members of the resistance were for the most part born on Aesgaard and had never been part in the wars of the old world. The resistance had been put in to place to make sure that you survived the wrath of your father, and hopefully, in extension place you on the throne. Everything had been perfect until the words of the prophecy had been burned in to the side of the mountain, Mount Aedelbra. It spoke of the death of the King at the hands of his son. Of course we didn't know which son as he had three. But the King showed his hand by going after you, and only you. Your brothers were spared. The many attempts on your life caught the attention of a group of powerful nobles, amongst which I was probably one of the most powerful and prominent. I am Duke Ull of the Van, at your service.* The Duke bowed to me. *We managed to get your two brothers over on our side and they agreed to help keep you alive and stop the prophecy from coming true. At first they weren't convinced that the prophecy hadn't been written with one of them in mind. However your father's actions soon made them see that it was you that was the true target of your father. Perhaps he knew something that no one else knew. There had been whispers you see, I don't know how much of the whispers were true. The whispers spoke of your brothers not truly being your brothers. The whispers spoke of them as being copies of you. I don't know if that was true or not. And if it was true, how it had been possible. I sent out some of my agents to find out, but couldn't find any evidence of them being either copies or brothers of yours. It was almost as if they hadn't existed in the first place. Anyways… The fateful day that the arrow hit your head, we had our people out watching over you. You rode hard and you rode fast on your favourite Sleipner to your favourite place at the waterfall. Our people had difficulties keeping up with you. Then, all of a sudden, without any warning an arrow came out of, seemingly, nowhere and struck your head. You fell off the Sleipner and hit the ground with a loud thud. By the time our people reached you, you were almost as good as dead. They got you back to the Palace. This was a mistake, they should have brought you back to our headquarter, that way we could have nursed you back to health and continued our clandestine war against your father and his tyrannical rule. Instead our hand was tipped and we had to reveal ourselves in order to rescue you. Your brothers came up with the plan that saved you. Avatar would lead us in to a battle with the loyalist troops in the hopes of drawing out your father. It worked, he left your side and led his troops against us. That gave your brother, Boris, the chance to get in to your room and get you out. We had a long-distance space ship waiting close by the Palace. Boris got you onboard and made it off-planet. Your father didn't waste any time once he found out what had happened. He sent off three space fighter ships in pursuit. Neither you nor they were seen again. Well at least not until your return now of course.* He smiled at me. *The loyalist troops started rounding us up and your brother, Avatar, managed to make his escape along with some other members of the resistance. He made it to another planet and has apparently created some kind of force of guardians as part of a defence against any offensive made by your father.* I didn't want to tell him the whole truth of what my brother had done since leaving Aesgaard, instead I just nodded and said that he had been keeping busy since leaving here. Duke Ull suddenly looked up in to the sky in the direction behind me. I turned to look at what he was looking at. Again I was having difficulties seeing what he was looking at, but then I saw them. At first they were only small dots on the sky, but then they started to grow in size and I could see them for what they were, the missiles. My father hadn't wasted any time. Now there was no doubt of whose story was the truth. I had paid for my stupidity with my life. There would be no survivors once the planetoid hit The Mesh. When the missiles hit the planetoid the whole place shook. Then there was nothing. I looked at Ull and the other men of the resistance. They in turn looked at me and at each other. There was an eerie silence as we all looked at each other, trying to gauge the situation. Had the explosions been enough to move the planetoid out of orbit or not? Then the entire planetoid started to move and make creaking noises. The orbit had been ruptured, we would soon be heading towards The Mesh and nothing could save us. I asked Ull how long time he reckoned that we would have before we hit The Mesh. *It all depends, if the planetoid continues like this, then*

we should have a few days of slow dying. But losing our orbit like
this may inflict some other gravitational forces on us before we
even reach The Mesh. We might be pulled apart long before then.
And once we reach it, the rest of us will be pulled apart, or utterly
pressurised. It doesn't matter what happens, the outcome will be
the same. We will be dead either in a matter of hours, or in a
matter of days.

I couldn't help but think about the old films from Earth's past. The
type of films where the hero ended up in trouble and everything
seemed bleak, but then from out of nowhere the cavalry, in
whatever form, arrived and saved the day. The thing about films
though, is that anything can happen, you kind of expect a happy
ending. The thing about real life though, is that anything can
happen, however you can't always expect a happy ending. There
would be no cavalry rushing in at the final moment before we all
die and rescue us. Not a chance. But yet… but yet… There was a
sound that was rising in volume. It sounded like the engine of a
space ship. It sounded like… I turned to look around at where the
sound was coming from and saw The Hermitage Shanks swoop in
from the sky. The door opened and William urged me to come
aboard quickly. I urged Ull and the other members of the resistance
to get onboard, then I got on. The door was closed and The
Hermitage Shanks swooped away from the planet. As we pulled
away from the planet, Ull's prediction of the gravitational forces
came true as the planetoid was suddenly pulled apart. So much for
the cavalry not arriving in the last moment in real life. William told
me that he had just been leaving with The Hermitage Shanks as he
had seen the missiles being fired towards The Cliff. He convinced
Flush to come to my rescue. Flush hadn't had to be convinced too
much, he thought the Universe would be better off with me alive
than dead.

The Hermitage Shanks sped away from the doomed planetoid, past
Aesgaard on our way to the shield and the way back to my
brother's planet. My brother had been worried that me coming here
would lead to war. He had been right. War was coming now and it
was my fault. If I wouldn't have come here in the first place, my

father wouldn't have known that I was still alive. As it is now, he will soon be rallying his troops to give chase. His entire fleet wouldn't be far behind. We had to reach my brother as soon as possible and get everyone prepared for the coming war. As we sped past Aesgaard the ship's radar picked up several small blips. Flush keyed a few sequences on the panel in front of him and brought up a visual of the blips. There were seven fighter ships hot in pursuit. It would be safe to say that they were probably armed to the teeth. I asked Flush what type of weapons The Hermitage Shanks had. Flush laughed *Our only weapon is Hermitage.* I asked what his powers were. Flush laughed again. *Don't you remember the incident with the rogue asteroid from my story? Hermitage's greatest power is his stench. Perhaps it will be powerful enough to repel these ships as it did with the asteroid.* So no weapons. How would we manage to survive this? Not only did we have the fighters on our tail, but we also had the shield to contend with. No matter how valid the licence is, if not revoked already, would they open up the shield and let us out. We were trapped. Then a thought hit me. The thought turned in to an idea and the idea in to a plan. A one in a million chance plan, but nonetheless a plan. I urged Flush to speed us along to the shield as fast as he could. Flush tried to argue that we would not be able to get out, but I quietened him and repeated my request. He shrugged and did as I bid. The fighters were still after us, not close enough to fire upon us yet, but still gaining on us. Would we reach the shield before they got in to range? My plan hinged upon us reaching the shield before the fighters came in to range.

Flush pushed the ship to its capacity and we could soon the shield far away in the distance. I soon saw what I was looking for and told Flush to steer the ship to the position that I pointed out to him, turn the ship around and grind it to a halt. Flush looked at me, unsure of what good that manoeuvre would do. William looked at me with a worried look on his face. *I hope you know what you are doing James.* I felt sweat trickling down my face from my forehead. I nodded slowly, but didn't reply. Flush got the ship in to my requested position. He grinded it to a halt. The seven fighters were all heading straight towards us, getting larger by the minute as they got closer to us. *Missiles!* Flush cried out. *They've all fired their missiles.* He looked up at me with a worried look on his face. *What now?* I asked him what type of missiles they were. Flush started to object, but the look on my face made him obey without question. He hit a few keys on the panel and got the result up on the screen. *They are heat seeking missiles. They have locked on to us as we are the hugest heat source out here, we haven't got a chance to outrun them.* Outrunning the missiles hadn't been my plan. I waited. The missiles closed in on us. When they were almost upon us, I ordered Flush to cut all the engines on the ship. Flush quickly did I as I had ordered him. No sooner had he switched off the engines did the missiles reach our position. But instead of hitting us, they veered over us and past us. My plan seemed to be working. A few more seconds… Then my plan yielded the result which I had hoped it would. The heat seeking missiles had locked on to the next source of heat in the vicinity, and that had happened to be one of the nodes in the shield. The node exploded and that section of the shield got closed down. Our way out had been guaranteed. Flush fired up the engines again and turned the ship around then steered it out through the shield's opening. *Wahoo!* He shouted out with glee! *That was a manoeuvre worthy of Flush Jordan himself. Hats off to you James Best!* We headed out through the shield but the threat was still not gone. The seven fighters were still on our tail and didn't seem to want to give up. *Now that we are free of the shields dampening effect we can send a message to your brother for some help.* Flush sent the message telling of the situation. We sped on towards my brother's planet with the fighters still gaining on us. I think everyone onboard was thinking the same thing, namely were we going to make it before the fighters get in firing-range of us again. They were gaining on us all the time. *Somebody call for the cavalry?* The voice came across the ship's radio and suddenly a dozen ships came from ahead of us and had soon passed over us on their way to infiltrate and engage the pursuing fighters. The pursuing fighters were taken by surprise and soon realised that retreating would be the better part of valour. The ships, that had been sent by my brother, then proceeded to escort us back to his planet.

Chapter 21

Upon reaching my brother's planet we found that he was already preparing for war. The blueprints that William had drawn up for him, on our first visit, of different types of warships had been handed to the shipbuilders and whilst we had been away they had been working around the clock. The fleet was now more or less complete. About fifty huge frigates, including a flagship, made up the bulk of the armada. There were also battleships that could be used up in close quarters for boarding enemy ships. Probably the most important part of the fleet were the fighter carriers. These were huge hulks of machinery that housed thousands upon thousands of smaller one-person fighters, like the ones that had come to our rescue on our way here. My brother had also sent out summons to all the Guardians throughout the universe to rally to him to participate in the war. Yahwe and Lucifer were here, so were Arthur and all the knights of the round table. I couldn't see Merlin anywhere, but there were thousands upon thousands of Guardians present and being posted to the different ships in the fleet. I got to be the pilot of one of the small fighter ships, so did William, Arthur and all the knights, and also Flush, amongst all the others. My brother had wanted me onboard the flag ship with him, but I told him that I would rather be in the middle of the action. He agreed to this, reluctantly.

Scout ships had been sent out in advance to find out when and where our father's fleet would be. It didn't take long for the scouts to discover the fleet. They were moving slowly towards us. My brother decided that we would ambush them at the planet Pulpone. The whole fleet was moved there to await our fathers' fleet.

We got the fleet in to position and awaited the coming of father's fleet. It didn't take too long for it to appear on our radars. *All pilots get to your fighters at once. Battle is imminent.* The female voice over the loudspeakers was brief and to the point. We all rushed to our ships to ready ourselves for the upcoming battle.

Sitting in the cockpit of the fighter ship, waiting for the battle to commence was tedious. I just wanted the klaxon to sound and the hangar doors to open so I could steer my ship out in to space and attack.

Still waiting… still waiting… still waiting. But then the klaxon sounded up. At first I didn't realise that the ear-piercing sound was actually the klaxon sounding for us to ready ourselves to exit the carrier and go forth in to battle. It wasn't until the hangar doors started to open, that I realised that this was it. The battle had started and we would be the first line in both the offensive and the defensive.

I started up the engine and steered my ship alongside the other fighters out through the open hangar doors to the awaiting battle that would soon be raging outside.

As all of our carrier ships spewed out fighters, so did the carrier ships of my father's fleet. This wouldn't be all too different from when I used to fly Hurricanes, back in World war II on Earth, in dog-fights with the German planes. No this wouldn't be too different at all. The difference would be that we were in space, we were in space fighters and there were thousands upon thousands of fighters on either side. So, no not any difference really. I had to start to focus on my flying and trying to discern which ships were enemy ones. It wasn't easy to see at first, but then I realised that William had designed an identifier computer onboard, which could tell apart friend from foe. That made things a whole lot easier. All I had to worry about was keeping my ship whole and as soon as an enemy ship was identified I would let lose a flurry of amplified light at it, then feeling the satisfaction as the ship went up in a silent explosion.

I soon lost count of all the enemy ships that I had silently blown up, but then I discovered that William had also designed a tally-keeper within the onboard computer. The computer told me that I had blown away three hundred and fifty two enemy ships all by myself. The computer also gave me data of what the others had tallied up, William for example had managed to tally up two hundred and forty one and Flush had tallied up five hundred and twelve. I needed to forget about the computer tally and focus on the enemy ships. I suddenly found myself close to one of the enemy's huge ships, I soon realised that it wasn't just a huge ship, it was the hugest of them all. Chances were that this ship was my father's flagship. I needed to chance everything to take him out, once and for all. No enemy fighters were in the vicinity, they all seemed to be keeping busy a good bit away from the flagship. This gave me the opportunity that I was looking for. I primed the missiles that my ship was carrying. It was armed with sixteen high-explosive missiles, which were designed to tear open steel. The walls of a huge flagship shouldn't pose any problems. I steered my ship towards the flagship, aimed my missiles at a portion of the ship and fired. All sixteen missiles flew away towards the flagship. Silent explosions showed me where they had impacted. Had they managed to make a hole? The smoke from the explosions cleared and I could see that the wall had a large gaping hole in it. I took my chance and steered my ship towards the hole.

Chapter 22

I had entered my father's flagship through the gaping wound in the side of it. I abandoned my own fighter in the corridor where I had crash-landed it. Troops were heading in my direction with their weapons at the ready. I drew out my sword and let the blade extract from the handle. I then let my sword do its speaking. I swung to the left and to the right. I swung the sword up and let it swoop down, I used it to slice my way through the hundreds of troops that had crammed in to the corridor with me. Stupid! I should have left someone alive so that I could have asked about the whereabouts of my father. I couldn't be sure that this ship was really his flagship, and if it was, was he onboard or still safe back on Aesgaard? I wouldn't put it past him to sit at home in safety while letting his people fight and die for him. But then again, I could be wrong. I ran down the corridor and came face to face with more troops. Again I let my sword do its talking. This time though, I made sure that I left one of the troops alive. When my sword had finished talking there was a badly wounded man lying on the floor. I went over to him, grabbed him and promised him quick and painless passing if he gave me the information that I wanted. The man groaned but soon let me know what I wanted. This was my father's flagship and he was onboard. With his dying breath he told me how I could get to where my father was. I was soon holding the lifeless man in my arms. I let him go and headed off in the direction that the man had told me my father would be.
Before I could reach my father the whole ship shook really badly. We were under attack. No, correction, my father was under attack. I would have to reach him, finish him off and get off this ship somehow, before my comrades managed to cause enough damage to actually destroy it.
I reached the bridge, where I had been told that my father would be. I wasn't disappointed. When I entered the bridge he was

standing in front of the huge bay window, looking at the battle. The bridge crew and my father were still not aware of my presence. I jumped up in the air and let my sword talk once again. The bridge crew did their best to stave off my attack, but it was all for naught. They fell to my sword as if they were trees being felled by a lumberjack. My father turned around in time to see the last of his bridge crew fall, dead, to the ground. He grimaced at me. Another blast from my brother's fleet shook the ship. My father didn't seem to notice, or perhaps it didn't bother him. He unsheathed his huge sword and walked slowly towards me. My sword looked like a toothpick in comparison. He lifted it over his head and swooped it down towards me, meaning to cleave me in half. I managed to step aside just in time. I swooped up my sword towards him and he easily parried it. Each time our swords made contact with each other it created a metallic song that would etch itself in to my mind forever. As we danced around each other, swiping and swooping our swords in the hopes of making contact with flesh, my brother's fleet was bombarding this ship, causing it to shake. After a number of direct hits, the ship started to tilt. I only noticed this when the floor that we had been dancing around on, started to lean. At first it didn't make much difference, but soon the tilt became too steep and we found ourselves dancing around on the walls of the ship as it made its way slowly but surely towards the gravitational pull of Pulpone. Both myself and my father continued to attack relentlessly and wouldn't allow for something as petty as the ship disintegrating around us put a stop to us. Our swords continuously met and made the metallic music. The ship was falling apart and had, unknown to myself and probably my father too, entered the gravitational pull of Pulpone. We were, with other words, going to crash. The ship's decline was now so big that we were dancing on the ceiling, more or less, but didn't let this stop us. This fight was going to be to the end, only one of us would walk away from this alive, and I was going to make sure that it was me. Now I started to notice that parts of the ship were being ripped off and there was an unnatural glow surrounding the entire ship, this was, I surmised, the ship burning up as it entered the planet's atmosphere. I decided that this would be my last chance to put a stop to my father, so I jumped up in to the air and swung my sword over my left shoulder, holding it with both my hands I let it swoop down towards my father as my jump brought me within striking distance. My father didn't even raise his sword to parry me away. Just as my sword sunk in to my father's head there was a loud metallic sound as the ship made contact with Pulpone's surface. I felt myself being thrust forward, still gripping my sword with both my hands it pried loose from my father's head and then darkness enveloped me.

To Be Continued…

Printed in Great Britain
by Amazon

17871025R00098